THE R

For years the Conde de Prados had been presumed dead. Now he had come back—relic of a lost world, figurehead of a lost cause, pretender to an impossible throne. What puzzled the CIA was why Prados, captured by the Russians in the Spanish Civil War, was permitted to return at all.

They sent their best man to find the answers. Dodging planted bombs and beautiful flamenco dancers, Peter Ward follows a trail of vicious killings as he attempts to discover whether Prados is really Prados . . . why a top Soviet agent has appeared in Madrid . . . and how an incredibly lovely infanta *figures in the ominous international storm that threatens the reign in Spain.*

Other SIGNET Thrillers You'll Enjoy

RETURN FROM VORKUTA

by David St. John

"There are the wolves . . . and then it is known you are an Englishman."

—ROBERT LOUIS STEVENSON
The Country of the Camisards

A SIGNET BOOK
Published by THE NEW AMERICAN LIBRARY

FIRST PRINTING, OCTOBER, 1965

SIGNET TRADEMARK REG. U.S. PAT. OFF. AND FOREIGN COUNTRIES
REGISTERED TRADEMARK—MARCA REGISTRADA
HECHO EN CHICAGO, U.S.A.

SIGNET BOOKS are published by
The New American Library, Inc.
1301 Avenue of the Americas, New York, New York 10019

PRINTED IN THE UNITED STATES OF AMERICA

Part I

He sat on the unyielding boards of the passenger-car bench, smelling the rank effluvia of crowded bodies, vodka, and the stench of the communal parasha *at the end of the car. Around him huddled ragged men, women, and babies, most of them like himself freed from* siblags*—the correctional labor camps of Russian Siberia—or from the* osoblager *—hard-regime camps like Magadan, Kolyma, and the Pechora mines.*

Survivors all, dehumanized, unreasoning creatures from a frozen underworld. Brutish troglodytes. Some with remnants of families waiting at stops along the way; others who would be met at the Potma redistribution center. And still others, like himself, who had no family at all in Russia.

With a piece of newsprint he rolled a cigarette of strong makhorka, *lighting it from a smoldering wick that passed from hand to hand among the passengers. Those who did not smoke dipped into cones of sunflower seeds purchased at Ukhta, the last train stop.*

Unlike his squat Slav companions he was tall, but in common with them his face wore the grained evidence of emaciation. Deep-set eyes and a falcon nose set him apart from the native Russians, and as he studied their stolid faces his hand lifted and touched a deep scar that slashed down across his cheekbone from the corner of his right eye. It was a mark, a physical alteration, which saved him from the faceless anonymity of existence in the siblags. KF 728 his number had been. Kontrik * *KF 728: survivor of two wars; Lubianka, Lefortovo, and Butyrki prisons; Userda, Novostroika, and finally Vorkuta—the siblags where he had spent twenty years of his life, twenty wasted years that had ground away young manhood and left him in middle age.*

His eyes peered through the steamed window at the frozen steppes beyond. Here in the white wasteland there was no

* Political prisoner sentenced under Article 58.

timbering operation, no Khrushchev corn sprouting in the vechnaya merzlota, *the permafrost zone whose soil was frozen as deep as seven hundred meters. The* merzlota, *he thought, the endless white* prostor *whose only living inhabitants were wolves and slave laborers and their wolflike guards.*

Across from him an old woman carefully unwrapped a rag bundle, her thin fingers plucking scraps from it furtively, protectively, as though camp blatnyaki *were watching her hungrily, ready to ravage the very crumbs of her hoard.*

It had been months since he had known gut-deep hunger, perhaps a year since he had snarled and battled with the volkovoy *for his share of* balanda, *the watery potato-cabbage soup that was the siblag staple; but he could remember the razor pains of hunger, the delirious fantasies of starvation that seized him in his bunk, or when he was staggering with the logging detachment through frozen forest. He remembered the fact and the delirium of hunger as though it had been only yesterday, and he knew that for the rest of his life those images would remain. Cold, starvation, and inhumanity had dulled his mind so that he could not remember all things well, and some things he could not remember at all. But the memory of hunger was as indelibly fixed as the cave paintings at Altamira, as the graven inscriptions on the Gothic citadels of Andalucía.*

At the sight of the woman eating he had begun to salivate unwittingly, unwillingly, for he had eaten well at Ukhta, and he would eat again when the train reached Kotlas. It might not be that night, but the knowledge that food awaited him at Kotlas was almost as good as devouring it.

Glancing down at his hand, he saw that unconsciously he had cupped it around the cigarette as though to shield it from the Siberian wind, to keep the savor of the smoke for his nostrils alone. There were new habits he would have to acquire, he told himself, a new way of living to adjust to, rich, nourishing food that his stomach might rebel against at first. All that, and another language to return to, to recall. In Madrid they would make allowances for his halting speech, his unfamiliar accent. . . . But he was racing ahead of himself.

Slowly, old boy, he said half aloud. Slowly—not everything at once. Everything by stages. In three days' time you have come from beyond the Arctic Circle to Pechora and Ukhta. Tomorrow you will see Kotlas and the next day Kirov. Then Gorky and finally Moscow.

To reassure himself he pressed the pocket of his coat and felt the crackle of documents: the train ticket, his labor card, remission-of-sentence certificate, food coupons, and the rubles he had saved as a volyne*—a so-called free worker outside Vorkuta's compound.*

In Moscow he would be entitled to a hotel room, to the unimaginable luxury of hot baths, coffee, and pastry, as much and as often as he desired. He would get new clothes—clean clothes—and some kind of travel document, perhaps a passport. The details were no longer clear in his mind. But there was time ahead to absorb what the camp official had told him, time in which everything would be explained again, made understandable. . . .

*Ex-*kontrik *KF 728 smoked his cigarette until the glowing end burned his fingers. Then he extinguished the tobacco with a drop of spittle and sifted the unburned flakes into his* makhorka *pouch.*

*A baby cried, two ex-*volyniki *burst into a loud dispute, and a trainman entered the compartment with whisk broom and pan to sweep up the littered husks of sunflower seeds from among the shabby felt boots of the travelers.*

Across the blinding prostor *the train jerked and labored toward Kotlas on the Severnaya Dvina River.*

ONE

Floating on his back, Peter Ward contemplated not his navel but the ceiling of the old octagon shed that sheltered Warm Springs pool. Whitewashed timbers radiating out from the apex resembled the ribs of an open umbrella, and Peter reflected that parasols had been fashionable for many of the two hundred years that the spa and its crude shelter had attracted the gentry of Virginia and the nearby East.

The 96 degree water was so clear as to give an illusion of shallowness, but at the center the spring was seven feet deep, the bottom strewn with smooth algae-covered stones that were pleasurable to stand and rest on. The Air Force general was doing so, but the manufacturer from Toledo was supporting himself on the surface rope and listening to the elderly attendant wheeze a lament of backstairs intrigue and kitchen treachery that accounted for his demotion from section maître in The Homestead dining room to his current situation as master of the Warm Springs shed. The old attendant coughed, and the scent of bourbon wafted gently through heated air and dispersed over the water.

Turning over, Peter surface-dived and skimmed over the ovaloid stones, swimming the rounded confines of the pool until his air gave out, and when he surfaced he saw the Toledo man toweling himself in one of the compartments while the Air Force general removed his wristwatch and dropped it into the water.

His audience gone, the attendant blinked at the general, who was staring fixedly at the bottom of the pool. Suddenly the general gave a grunt of satisfaction, disappeared under the surface, and reappeared with his watch.

"Testing?" Peter asked.

"That's right." He fitted the strap around his wrist and began climbing out of the spring. "They claimed you could read the engraving on a coin at the bottom, but hell, the water's clearer than that: I could tell the time." Taking a towel from the attendant, he stalked into a compartment and closed the door.

Peter said, "What time is it, Marco?"

" 'Bout three, suh. Say—how you know my name?"

"I remember you," Peter told him, "from the old days."

"The old days?" A grin spread over his face. "How old, suh?"

"Twenty years ago." Peter breaststroked toward the underwater steps. "I used to come here with my parents. Remember Dr. Ward?"

"Certainly do, suh. My, my, how the time goes by. Dr. and Mrs. Ward. Table twenty-six. Every Thanksgiving, was it?"

"Every Easter," Peter corrected, reaching for a towel.

"You by youse'f now, Mr. Ward? Or you wife swimmin' in the ladies' part?"

"I'm a widower," Peter told him, and was glad to hear the ring of the telephone.

From the general's compartment came a bellow. "If that's SAC, tell them I'm not here. I'm on vacation."

"I hear you, Gen'ral," Marco called, and vanished into his room.

Before Peter could turn on the cold shower, Marco was rapping on his door. "For you, Mr. Ward. Long distance, suh."

Draping a towel around his hips, Peter padded over the planking into Marco's room. He picked up the phone and said, "Peter Ward."

"Mr. Ward? Thank you," the operator said. Then to the caller, "I have your party, Mr. Bottomley."

Mr. Bottomley, Peter winced, and heard the precise and modulated voice of his chief, Avery Thorne.

"Peter?" Thorne said cheerfully. "Where are you?"

"About five miles from The Homestead."

"In what condition?"

"Naked. You will have your little jape, Mr. Bottomley."

"Telephone discipline, Peter," Thorne said blandly. "Naked, you say?"

"It's the custom at Warm Springs."

"Very agreeable, too. Relaxing after an active day?"

"I rode for an hour before breakfast, shot skeet afterward and a fast eighteen by lunch." He cleared his throat. "I'm supposed to be on leave, Chief. One week—of which three days remain."

"Afraid you're recalled, Peter."

"As of when?"

"As of now. I want you to get dressed, pack up, and settle your bill."

Peter swallowed. "It's a five-hour drive to Washington, a good part of it over mountain roads. Even pushing I can't get there before eight tonight."

"To circumvent that difficulty I'm sending a plane for you. Ingalls Field, isn't it?"

"Very thoughtful. Yes, it's Ingalls Field. What time?"

"The plane's airborne now. Say four fifteen."

"Any likelihood I'll be able to come back and finish my leave?"

"Practically none. This involves foreign travel."

"I see. Care to give me a clue?"

Thorne paused before replying. Then, "You can take along my measurements for Pascal."

"Pascal," Peter repeated musingly. It was the name of a tailor he had used occasionally in Madrid. "Where do we meet? Langley?"

"No, I'm giving a dinner tonight at the Chevy Chase Club for one of the Middle East liaison types. Why don't you take a room at Bradley House and I'll meet you there? That will give us a drink together before my hosting duties start, then afterward you'll be handy."

"Whatever you say," Peter said glumly, and hung up.

Beside him Marco said, "Bad news, suh?"

"I have to go back to Washington."

The old attendant cluck-clucked. "You a doctor like you fathah?"

"No, a lawyer." He took a second towel from Marco, showered in his compartment, and dried off briskly. When he was dressed he signed a chit, tipped the attendant, and walked out to where he had parked the rented Lancia, wondering what urgent CIA business was dispatching him to Madrid. For how long? he wondered. Overnight? A week? A year? There was one thing to be said of Avery Thorne, Deputy Director and Chief of the Clandestine Services—he played his cards very slowly. No shock treatment from the urbane Avery, just gradual disclosure of an operational plan—so gradual that by the time revelation was complete the most *outré* mission seemed totally logical and feasible. Had Thorne chosen private life rather than government service he would have made a superb salesman or advocate.

Peter started the engine, buttoned his car coat, and backed around to the road. The time was early spring, but spring came late in the mountains, and patches of dirty snow could still be seen on the surrounding hills. He followed the winding road back to The Homestead, envying a group of golfers their afternoon round as he passed the eighth hole.

After a four-month operation along the bleak Ladakh frontier Peter had assumed Thorne would honor his minimal week's leave, but that illusion had been erased by Thorne's peremptory summons.

When he reached Hot Springs, Peter turned the Lancia

over to the car rental office and climbed the slanting path to The Homestead's side entrance. At the desk he asked to have his bill prepared, then went to his room and packed. That done, he phoned the stables and canceled the horse he had reserved for the next morning, went down into the lobby and paid his bill. A porter with his luggage joined him on the front steps and saw him into a taxi.

Madrid, he thought, as the taxi left Hot Springs and headed for the town's small airport. I haven't heard of any crisis brewing in Spain. Then he pushed speculation from his mind, since in a few hours Avery Thorne would brief him on his new assignment.

The plane that landed was a Beechcraft Queen Air, and when the pilot climbed out Peter saw he was Fred Harkins. Carrying his bags over to the plane, Peter shoved them into the luggage compartment. Harkins said, "Rough deal, Peter. Sorry I have to be the instrument of woe."

"That's Potomac Plumbing for you," Peter said resignedly. He got into the plane and was easing into a seat when Fred invited him to fly copilot. Peter strapped himself in, activated the radio, and fitted on earphones. Harkins said, "What's the chief got for you?"

"He didn't say—telephone discipline."

"Yeah—I shouldn't even be asking." Harkins switched on the ignition and started the port engine, one of twin 340 HP Lycomings. "Anyway, it's lousy luck. Think you'll miss squadron reunion?"

"I suppose so." They had known each other as Marine aviators in the Korean War, and the annual reunion of their fighter squadron was a sacrosanct event. "You'll have to drink my share, Fred."

Harkins grunted. "Not much chance of that. Oka-san won't let me." Running up the starboard engine, he called the tower for clearance and steered the plane toward the end of the runway.

As Peter lowered flaps, Harkins said, "I'm still not used to civilian flying. I feel naked without my oxygen mask."

Peter nodded reminiscently.

"Well," Harkins said, "here we go, old buddy. Wheels up for Disneyland East."

They flew up the Shenandoah Valley, over the Blue Ridge Mountains, and with Warrenton in sight, Peter throttled back and circled down over Southlands, the Fairfax County estate that belonged to his sister and her husband. Horses, Suffolks, and Herefords grazed over the faintly greening landscape below.

"Just what I'd like to have," Harkins said enviously. He called National Airport tower and headed the plane south of Alexandria while Peter lowered flaps and landing gear.

Outside the terminal building a car waited, a black one with an inconspicuous antenna. Peter got into it and said, "Chevy Chase Club," to the driver, who touched the visor of his cap, lifted the radio mike, and repeated the destination to the CIA dispatcher.

Outward-bound traffic was in full cry, but the northbound lanes were almost empty, and the driver took Memorial Bridge into the Federal City, following Connecticut Avenue to the northwest limit of the District, where the club's nearly two hundred gently rolling acres began.

Scott, the Negro doorman, welcomed Peter and told him that his secretary had reserved a room for him in Bradley House.

Peter smiled faintly at the subtle Thorne touch: to avoid any association between an overt and a covert element of the agency, Thorne had had his secretary pass the word to Peter's secretary, Miss Armistead, installed in Peter's cover law office. Miss Armistead, then, had made the reservation call to the club, where her voice and name were known.

A porter carried Peter's bags through the clubhouse proper and into the adjoining lodge for transient guests. Bradley House was one of the club's older buildings, with rooms comfortably if not sumptuously furnished. In the hall hung flintlocks and naval models, fading prints of the old Chevy Chase Hunt, and photographs of Presidents Taft and Eisenhower on the putting greens.

Peter noticed that the rooms on either side of his were unoccupied. When the porter had left, he opened the window blind and looked out over the dusk-hung links, the rows of shrubbery and well-placed groves in the distance.

After opening his bags he showered, changed into a clean shirt, and ordered drinks from the bar. He thought of calling Patty Allard for a late date, then realized he could well be tied up with Thorne until early morning. Peter broke out his pipe, filled it with Middleton 5, and was measuring water into his Canadian Club when he heard a light rapping at his door. "Peter?"

The door opened inward on Avery Thorne, his tall, slim frame garbed in dinner jacket.

"The Jolly Green Giant," Peter greeted him.

"Hello, Seraph," Thorne said as they shook hands. "Still nettled?"

"Moderately." He indicated the drink tray. Thorne went to it and built a weak Scotch, then turned to Peter. "The reason I hauled you back is because I'm leaving in the morning for two weeks in the Far East."

"I always assume you have your reasons."

Thorne sipped his drink and nodded. Sitting in an easy chair, he looked up at Peter. "By the time I get back you'll be gone."

"Madrid, you indicated."

"Yes, Madrid." He reached for the ice bowl and added a cube to his glass. "It's a curious case, Peter. There may be nothing to it, but it also may turn out to be a significant move by the Sovs."

"Deception?"

"Possibly." He ran one hand through his fine, entirely white hair. "Jim Hopwood will give you details tomorrow, but I wanted some time to sketch the broad picture and possibly suggest an operational approach."

Laying down his pipe, Peter sipped his drink and waited.

Thorne glanced at his wristwatch. "Know anything about Spanish politics?" he asked.

Peter shrugged. "More than some, less than others."

Thorne's youthful eyes twinkled. "I thought the Seraph was infallible."

"Hardly."

"Then to refresh your memory, General Primo de Rivera retired from the dictatorship of Spain in 1930. Elections were held the following year, and the parties of the monarchy were defeated. King Alfonso XIII went into exile. In 1936, the army revolted against the leftist-anarchist government, and after military intervention on both sides the issue was finally settled in 1939. Between half a million and a million Spaniards were killed in the Civil War. The pretender—Don Juan, Count of Barcelona—remains in exile at Estoril, and his son, Prince Juan Carlos, may be the next king of Spain—if the Regency Council selects him following Franco's death, as now seems likely." He paused to sip from his glass. Peter said nothing.

"That's part of the background," Thorne continued, and glanced across at the dark window. "The current part is of more interest to us. In the Spanish Civil War international communism was defeated for the first—and I might say only—time, in a military conflict. The Communists have never forgotten, much less forgiven, although a lot of the principal actors on the Communist side have since been disgraced, executed, or simply vanished from sight. A smooth and constitutional transition from Franco will hardly suit their purposes. As you well know, communism blooms best in situations of chaos and anarchy, social turmoil and violence. We have important bases in Spain—NATO bases for SAC and the Navy, even though socialist Scandinavia and Belgium won't admit Spain to membership. So we—our government—has a vested interest in Spanish political stability."

"Spain's internal politics haven't changed appreciably in years," Peter commented. "Where's the sudden threat? Not from the Republican exiles, surely. The ones who fled to Moscow are still there for the most part, the rest scattered through a dozen countries, largely absorbed in bourgeois pursuits like making money."

"True," Thorne said, "except for one unmentioned factor: resistance to the Law of Succession on the part of the Royalists. The Carlists and Royalists," he went on, sitting forward, "gave as much blood as anyone in the Civil War, but afterward they were ignored by Franco. Politically they don't exist in today's Spain—except that they *do* exist, and they don't want to see Alfonso's grandson on the throne. Do you recall the origins of the dispute?"

"Only faintly."

Thorne glanced at his watch again and said, "Its roots are in the nineteenth century, following the political upheavals of the Peninsular War. The Royalists claim that the then Count of Prados should have inherited the vacant throne through his father, the dead king's brother. Instead, the count's cousin, son of the dead king's sister, was crowned, and promptly repealed the law which, until then, specifically forbade succession through the female line. The count's followers rose and embarked on a war that lasted more than a decade. Finally concessions on both sides brought an end to the Royalist insurrection, and a détente lasted through the Spanish Civil War more than a century later. Now, with Franco aging and the Prince of Asturias the leading contender for the post-Franco throne, the Royalists are getting restless."

"Not to mention the natives. Do the Royalists have an alternate to offer?"

"They do. His name is Don Jaime Rodrigo Pérez y Vals Salvat, Count of Prados. In the Spanish Civil War he was one of the leaders of the Royalist brigades; later he was a colonel in the Blue Division at Novgorod, where he was captured by the Russians." Thorne stood up. "I'll drop back about midnight, Peter."

Rising, Peter said, "The Russians captured him and let him go?"

"Apparently so," Thorne said, walking toward the door. "He was released from the Vorkuta Siblag a few weeks ago and just reached Madrid."

Peter opened the door for his chief. "He must have incredible powers of survival."

Thorne smiled faintly. "Incredible is the word, Peter. Our information—from half a dozen sources—has been that the Count of Prados died in Vorkuta some twenty years ago."

TWO

There was not much point, Peter thought, in trying to reconcile the paradoxical aspects of Thorne's story, since the Chief of the Clandestine Services was returning to amplify his remarks; either the Vorkuta returnee was the vanished count or he was not. So Peter went down to the dining room, where he ate squab stuffed with chestnuts, enjoyed a dry Graves, and then wandered into the bar, wondering why Thorne had selected him for this particular assignment. As he passed the Queen of Clubs that marked the club's inviolate male area, he saw some friends around one of the tables and joined them. One was a congressman, another a columnist, the third a space agency official.

They shook dice for their brandies and argued domestic and world politics until eleven, when the group broke up: the columnist heading for his typewriter, the NASA man for Cape Kennedy, and the congressman for his home. Peter called for a pot of black coffee and the morning paper, and finished both by a quarter to twelve.

As he walked through the nearly deserted clubhouse, his mind returned to Thorne's subject and its veiled implications, and when he was back in his room he lighted his pipe and considered a number of possible approaches until Thorne knocked on the door and came in.

Opening his tie and collar, Thorne sank back in a chair and said, "Glad *that's* over. Fortunately, Farkas is orthodox Moslem, so there was none of the interminable and alcoholic toasting." He drew one hand across his forehead. "Had time to ponder our little conundrum?"

"I've been trying not to."

Thorne frowned. "That's not like you."

"Mind telling me how my name came out of the hat?"

"Simple. We needed a senior operations officer who spoke Spanish, could move comfortably through several strata of Spanish society, and—was available."

Peter grunted. "There must have been a dozen to pick from."

"One additional factor, Peter—access to the target."

Peter blinked. "What kind of access do I have to Spanish Royalists—to the Conde de Prados in particular?"

Thorne sat forward, sighed, and lighted a cigarette. "You

underestimate the Squirrel System. Electronic data retrieval is becoming the heart of our business." Exhaling smoke, he sat comfortably back. "Remember a Professor Carberry? Professor J. S. Carberry?"

"I had some classes with him in pre-law."

"Odd type, I gather."

"Chimerical."

Thorne chuckled. "Squirrel clicked and chattered, lights glowed, and behold—Carberry's name popped out."

"In what connection?"

"His avocation—researching the juridical basis of monarchies past and present."

Peter sucked on his pipe. "I remember him—unbuttoned coat and trailing scarf heading untidily down College Hill. Some said his feet never touched the ground."

"Be that as it may," Thorne said in a chiding tone, "Carberry has access to the Royalists—and through him so have you."

"He must be emeritus by now."

"He is, but he keeps up a lively correspondence with an old colleague of his, Professor Eduardo Sainz, who maintains the Royalist archives in Madrid. Now," said Thorne, rising and moving toward the window, "let's go back to what I told you before dinner. First, the Count of Prados has been presumed dead so conclusively that his daughter was granted his title. Second, the Count of Prados now in Madrid arrived in Moscow from Vorkuta and immediately applied for a Swedish passport, Spain not having diplomatic relations with the U.S.S.R. We learned about it shortly before the reporters did and ran his name through Squirrel, dredging up all that I've told you so far. Obviously, if the man in Madrid isn't the count he's an impostor and very likely a KGB * plant." Thorne pivoted and faced Peter. "You're wondering why it can't be proved one way or another? Well, if you'll recall, during the Civil War the Reds delighted in destroying files and records, for personal and ideological reasons. They burned police files, military records, and every civil register they could lay their hands on. They also sacked the Prados mansion in Madrid. The anarchists in particular—the CNT—tried to obliterate every tangible evidence of the existence of their class enemies, make un-persons of them. In many cases they succeeded abundantly."

The telephone rang. Peter answered it and heard a voice say quietly, "Mr. Ward? Is Avery with you?"

"Yes, sir." To Thorne he said, "Sounds like the director."

* Komitet Gosudarstvennoy Bezopasnosti—Committee for State Security (organization for nonmilitary intelligence).

Thorne took the phone, and while he talked Peter refilled his pipe and poured a mild Canadian Club. The call over, Thorne said, "I'm to stop by his house on my way to the airport." He lighted a cigarette and resumed.

"In the face of that calculated destruction, there may well be no documents that can either support or disprove the count's identity."

"The Royalist archives? Professor Sainz?"

"Station personnel have already gone over everything he has, and there's nothing that would identify one individual as against another. Some of the archives were destroyed in 1937, and the remainder deal with the stream of Royalist history rather than the physical characteristics of persons." He knocked ash from his cigarette. "Care to take over the Madrid station, Peter?"

Peter shook his head. "Once I'd have welcomed it, Avery, but not anymore. I've had enough of embassies and diplomatic life. It was in Cairo that my wife was killed, when I was under embassy cover, and the circumstances are hard to forget. Besides, the daily demands of protocol—dinners, cocktails, and diplomatic entertaining—are so much wasted time. I want to spend my time usefully, Chief—not making out fitness reports, inventorying office supplies, and acting as a buffer to the ambassador so other people can get their jobs done."

"I sympathize with your outlook," Thorne said almost wistfully. "It's been a dog's age since I handled a real live agent, and I suppose I may never handle one again. I'm not an intelligence officer any longer—I'm only one more desk where papers pause in their endless procession."

"I wouldn't even want station contact," Peter said. "For this kind of job I'd prefer the station not be involved."

"I don't know—" Thorne said doubtfully, "but—"

"I've got access," Peter broke in, "through Carberry and Sainz. I don't need the embassy. Don't hang it around my neck."

"Well," Thorne sighed, "the Special Group knows about you. I suppose that will cover this case."

"I'd also like a Bigot List * maintained."

"All right, arrange it with Jim Hopwood; he'll be your case officer."

Peter bit down on his pipestem and gazed at Thorne. "I see it as a two-phase operation. First, establish the identity of the count. Then, if he isn't who he purports to be, what

* A controlled inventory of all persons knowledgeable in a particular field.

do we do? Tie the can on him or play him back against the Sovs?"

"Other things being equal I vote for playback—but other things are seldom equal. If we reach that stage we'll have to take another look—a long one. And if the Spanish Service gets wind of what you're involved in they'll take the play from you without a by-your-leave and execute the so-called count by sunup. You could even find yourself in a Spanish jail."

Peter massaged his throat lightly. "How are relations with the Spanish Service?"

"Generally good, but in some ways disappointing. Particularly in the case of the Niños—the thousands of Spanish Republican children who returned from Russia to Spain under the amnesty a few years back. Perhaps four thousand of them had been trained by the RIS for sabotage and propaganda and as sleeper agents. We helped identify them and hoped to double perhaps a hundred, but Spain's a different country now, bulging with prosperity, the Civil War studiously forgotten. The Spanish jailed or executed many of the identified agents and let others slip away unmolested to the hinterlands without even so much as routine police checks in their districts." He shook his head. "Among them may be the count's KGB contact, and if you can identify him, you'll be well on the way to uncovering the Soviet illegal *rezidentura* in Spain."

"If," Peter echoed. "If the count's a ringer."

"Yes," Thorne acknowledged. "Never assuming the improbable is impossible, that's where we start, Peter. What we have to begin with." His face looked strained, and Peter found himself marveling at Thorne's stamina. He had traveled abroad with his chief and found it a grueling endurance contest. He recalled the physical erosion of the flights and arrivals, station briefings, ambassadorial chats, station dinners that seemingly lasted all night. Then Thorne would dictate cables and memoranda for two or three hours, take a brief nap, and get up early for a flight to the next stop. . . .

"It could be quite a haul, Peter. You'll take the assignment, I presume."

Peter smiled. "Not that I have a choice. It's enough different from my usual line that I like it."

"And you'll forgive me your three days' unspent leave?" Thorne asked.

"That goes without saying."

Draining his glass, the Chief of the Clandestine Services stood up, stretched, and yawned. For Thorne, the legendary robot, it was an unusually human gesture.

"Hopwood's coming to your law office at ten o'clock in

the morning, Peter. I imagine he'll bring along the 201 on the count for a starter, possibly the Chief of the Spanish Desk. You'll have some reading to do on the *siblag* system, with emphasis on Vorkuta and other camps where the count reportedly was sent before his death, then a close examination of Spanish politics."

"How soon do you want me in Madrid?"

"As soon as you're prepared. We've had no prior dealings with Professor Carberry, so you'll have to massage him yourself." Bending over, he stubbed out his cigarette. "Oh, yes, I should have mentioned the Royalists' paramilitary organization. They're called Brigadas, and the leaders are veterans of the Civil War, the Blue Division, or both. They drill without arms, and two or three times a year meet en masse to be reviewed by their titular leader, the young Countess of Prados—if she's still called that."

"A *girl*?"

"Odd in a Latin country, isn't it? But you'll see photographs of her in khaki uniform and blue beret. With her father dead she represented the Royalists' last hopes, Peter. While she was still a very young child she was made the political queen bee of the movement. The Brigadas total an estimated fifteen thousand men, and if they were encouraged to assert their claims either before or after Franco dies a very ugly and violent situation could result—one playing directly into the Kremlin's hands. State's concerned, so are Defense and the Special Group." He smiled, and all traces of fatigue left his face. "I hope we can put their minds at rest."

As they shook hands Peter said, "Want that suit from Pascal?"

"Of course I do," Thorne said, "but this year I've got three offspring in college and I'm still paying for Nancy's debut. Good luck, Seraph." He left the room, and his passage down the hall was barely audible.

Finishing his drink, Peter undressed and got into bed, thinking he should have called his sister after dinner, and told Danny Choi he would be back in Georgetown after breakfast. Moonlight flooded his window, cold and lifeless, and for a moment Peter thought of snowbound camps in Siberia, the frosty breaths of slave laborers, the *Untermenschen* of the Communist system. Even the name Vorkuta meant underworld people, he reflected, and then his mind flashed across a continent to the arid plains of Estremadura, where a slight girl in blue beret and khaki uniform stood motionless before marching companies of leathery veterans who dipped their guidons in homage and salute. She would be thin-lipped, he thought, with imperious eyes and the austere stamp of aristocracy on her features. He thought of her father the count, and wondered how many repatriated Niños had joined the Royalist Brigadas—and to what purpose. Then he turned on his side and drifted off to sleep.

After breakfast in the grill Peter took a cab to his Georgetown house and carried his bags up the front steps. He rang and waited, but there was no response inside. He unlocked the door, entered, and saw a note lying on the hall table.

It was from Danny Choi, saying he had left early for the university library and expected to be back by five.

Lugging his bags upstairs, Peter remembered Danny as he had first seen him—a tattered, half-frozen Korean urchin, beckoning at him through the snow, leading him stumbling and half blind to the safety of Johnny Havas' CIA team. Another year and Danny would have his doctorate in linguistics; meanwhile, he worked as a simultaneous interpreter for State's international conferences and lived at Peter's house.

Peter opened his bags and changed into a medium-weight gray Urquhart suit, golf round collar, and Atkins brogues. Then he telephoned his sister.

"I hope you're still enjoying Hot Springs, Peter," she said.

"Wish I were, Anne, but Thorne sent the press gang for me."

"What a shame. Does it mean you're off again?"

"Eventually, but not Ladakh again. Madrid, the man said, and I've known worse places."

"An infinity of them, it seems to me."

"How are the children?"

"Fine. Will you be seeing us soon?"

"Probably not before the weekend. Some intensive studying to do."

"Is—will the assignment be dangerous?"

"Just driving on the freeway is dangerous."

"True, but—"

"Love to the children, Anne; regards to Eric."

"Thanks for calling, Peter."

Hanging up, he glanced at his watch, left the house, and walked over to Wisconsin Avenue in the cool, damp morning. At a car rental office he rented an Alfa-Romeo roadster and tried it out on Rock Creek Parkway as he headed toward upper Connecticut Avenue. Peter was in Washington so little that renting transportation was more convenient—and cheaper—than owning a car, with the additional advantage of no maintenance worries.

The legend on his office door said: "Peter Ward, Attorney-at-Law," an assertion substantiated by framed diplomas on the reception-room walls from Brown and Yale Law, and a membership certificate from the District Bar Association.

His secretary was nicely turned out in a light blue wool-knit suit. She stood up as he entered and said, "Good morning, Mr. Ward."

" 'Morning, Miss Armistead."

She flushed prettily. "What a shame you had to come back so soon. Did they have room for you at the club?"

"They did, thank you, and please sit down. I'm neither old enough nor important enough to rate your rising when I come in."

"I—" she began, her face reddened, and she sat down at her desk. "Mr. Hopwood will be here at ten."

"Hopefully. Jim can be a little casual about time." He hung his raincoat on the costumer, laid his hat on the rack, and went into his office.

"Coffee, Mr. Ward?" his secretary called.

"With pleasure." He sat behind his desk and began thumbing through the mail Miss Armistead had opened for him. There was an alumni ballot for Andover trustees, bills from a florist, Magruder's, the car rental agency, the Chevy Chase and University clubs. His secretary had made out checks for each, and he finished signing them as she came in with a thermal jug of hot coffee. She was an attractive young lady, he reflected, and wondered how long Headquarters would keep her isolated in his office, away from the mainstream of agency life, from contact with bright and elegible young officers and the junior trainees who were the cream of each June's graduating classes. Many girls had passed through his office portals, some staying as little as a week, others as long as six months. They liked it at first, because its location eliminated the long bus rides to and from Langley, but after a while the stretches of near solitude preyed on them until they asked for a change.

Pouring coffee for himself, Peter noticed that Miss Armistead had supplied extra cups for Hopwood and whomever he might bring to the meeting. He pressed the intercom button and said, "Miss Armistead, will you bring your pad?"

When she was seated beside him he said, "Letter to Dr. Josiah S. Carberry, Brown University, Providence, Rhode Island. Dear Dr. Carberry: Knowing of your continuing interest in the juridical basis of monarchies past and present, I am taking the liberty of requesting a letter of introduction from you to Professor Eduardo Sainz of Madrid. The reason underlying my request is a recent grant awarded me by the X Foundation, which—"

"The 'X Foundation,' Mr. Ward?"

"Cover will provide the name."

"I see." She made a marginal note and looked at him expectantly.

"Which," Peter continued, "is underwriting my stay in Europe for six months while I prepare a paper on certain legal aspects of monarchic succession. Professor Sainz is said to be an authority on Spanish Royalist affairs, and I should appreciate an opportunity to examine at least a part of his extensive archives. Other arrangements have been made for me in France, Italy, and Portugal, eliminating my having to turn to you for additional favors in those directions. With cordial regards."

"Clean draft?"

"Please. To show Hopwood."

Her nose wrinkled. "Is there really a Dr. Carberry?"

"We'll see if he replies," Peter said, and turned to see Hopwood enter, followed by a younger, redhaired man who carried a briefcase.

Miss Armistead showed them into the office, where Peter shook hands with the Western Europe chief. "Sorry to inconvenience you by meeting here, Jim. Nothing for efficiency, everything for security."

"Exactly," Hopwood grumbled. "You look fit, Peter. This is Sam Perkins. Sam, Mr. Ward."

The redhead grinned. "Good to meet you, sir. I've heard a lot about you."

"Sorry about that."

"You needn't be, sir."

Hopwood pulled off his coat, and lifted the briefcase onto Peter's desk while Perkins hung both coats on the costumer.

"He's a likely lad, Peter," Hopwood remarked. "Bilingual in Spanish and Catalan."

"How's his English?"

"Just fair," Hopwood said. "About like mine." He took a wooden-tipped cigarillo from his pocket and lighted it carefully. Then he eased his long body into a chair and gazed at Peter through thick, metal-framed round glasses. "Avery briefed you last night?"

"He outlined the problem."

They waited while Perkins brought in the audio-interrupter device from the file safe beside Miss Armistead's desk, set the metal box on Peter's desk, and plugged the cord into a wall outlet. The grilled side of the box gave off a warm orange glow. To their ears the electronic emanations were soundless, but not to a hidden mike.

As Perkins closed the door Peter said, "How'd you manage Catalan?"

"I was brought up in Barcelona, went to the university there."

"One of the advantages of expatriation," Hopwood observed. "Sam's a walking Iberian atlas." Opening the briefcase, he shoved some files at Peter. "The 201 file on our resurrected count, a paper on the Royalist Movement—somewhat out of date—and a bunch of debriefings provided by former slave laborers."

"Also," Perkins added, "traces on Professor Sainz."

Peter said, "We might title this project 'From Siberia to Iberia in Twenty Hard Years.' "

Hopwood grunted.

Miss Armistead came in and handed the Carberry letter to Peter, who passed a carbon to Hopwood. "You might drop this off with Cover when you get back, Jim. They'll have to provide the sponsoring foundation."

"You aren't going to be a hotel wallah this trip?"

"This time I'm an intellectual, third class."

"Ad astra per aspera," Hopwood intoned, and tucked the letter carbon into a pocket. Drawing the cigar from his mouth, he blew smoke toward the window. "So much for preliminaries," he said. "Let's get on with the job, Peter. I'm due back at the Joss House by noon."

THREE

Until the weekend Peter worked in quiet concentration. Then he relaxed at Southlands, riding Kuro, his black hunter, in company with Anne and her children, Robin and Kyle. Shelagh, his German shorthair, usually preceded the riders, flushing quail and pheasant from the cover of hedgerows. Sunday evening Peter returned to his Georgetown house, changed to black tie for the National Symphony, and in the morning reached his office ahead of the punctual Miss Armistead.

A letter postmarked Providence waited for him, a letter from Dr. Carberry that began "Dear Ward" and went on to express the professor's gratification over Peter's grant from the Blackstone Foundation and his coming research in Spain. He had sent a letter to Professor Sainz in Madrid, carbon enclosed, describing Peter in flattering terms and assuming the unqualified cooperation of Professor Sainz. In return, Carberry requested a copy of Peter's treatise after publication.

Peter felt uneasily guilty over deceiving old Carberry, and when his secretary came in he dictated a note of appreciation. Since no paper would ever be drafted, much less published, Peter decided to send the professor something he might prize—an illuminated palimpsest from the monastery at Burgos or San Juan de la Peña, possibly a Colonial Codex, or some Etruscan ceramics. The agency could afford the tab.

"I saw you at the concert last night," Miss Armistead told him.

"Sorry I missed seeing you."

"I don't know how you could have seen us. We were high up in the second balcony."

"We?"

She colored slightly. "My roommate and I. After seeing you she asked me for first chance at my job if—when—I leave."

"Is she an agency employee?"

"She works for Senator Bradley."

"I see. Are you planning to transfer?"

"No, I—I mean I won't have anything to say about it."

"The job can't be much fun," Peter said sympathetically. "At least you get a chance to read while I'm away."

"There's hardly a magazine I don't subscribe to, Mr. Ward, and I'm leading my philosophy class."

"Are you studying for an advanced degree?"

"Only some night courses at George Washington Extension. And I wouldn't be doing that if life were—well, a little more interesting."

The standard complaint of the government secretary, Peter reflected, briefly regretting the tradition of not getting involved with your own secretary. He wondered if Sam Perkins was married or knew any bachelor officers.

The telephone rang and Peter answered, hearing the voice of Chick Brandeau, playing manager of the Potomacs amateur hockey team. "Peter? We're in a bind again and I hope you can help out."

Peter had been right wing on the Brown team that retired the Ivy League cup, and played occasionally with the Potomacs. "What's the problem, Chick?"

"Schuyler has a bad knee from the St. Nick's game. The doc says he can't play against Philadelphia, and we're hoping you can fill in."

"When's the game?"

"Saturday night."

Peter shook his head. "I wish I could, Chick, but I'll be out of town. I won't even be in the country."

"Too bad!" the manager said dejectedly. "I was sort of counting on you, Peter, so if your plans change and you don't leave, I wish you'd let me know."

"I will, Chick—and I'm sorry." Hanging up, he frowned, and the fingers of his right hand unconsciously touched the bridge of his nose with its light tracery of puck-and-stick scars. He would have liked nothing better than hitting the ice again with the Potomacs; two of his classmates were regulars on the team.

To Miss Armistead he said, "Lev Kowalski still due at nine thirty?"

"Yes, sir. At least, he hasn't canceled the appointment." Picking up her pad, she left the office.

Kowalski was on loan from the visible portion of the agency iceberg. He was an expert on the Soviet correctional labor system and the jargon and argot of the Siberian camps, one of the many anonymous specialists dedicated to collating intelligence on one small and esoteric portion of the Soviet spectrum. If the practice of intelligence was anything, Peter mused, it was far from an individual effort. Many hands, an unknown number, went into perfecting the final brew, from secret-writing chemists and researchers, disguise and cover technicians, ordnance experts and scuba divers to men who fed the electronic maw of the huge Squirrel index-and-retrieval system. There was no known art unpracticed within CIA, and many clandestine ones as well.

Picking up the telephone, Peter called the Foxhall Road home of Patty Allard and learned from the maid that Mrs. Allard was at her Zihuatanejo villa and not expected back for at least another month. The idle rich, Peter murmured as he hung up, and reflected that Patty was at least one divorcée who knew the enjoyment of wealth. Because of her absence his last days in Washington would be celibate.

Before Kowalski arrived Peter telephoned the Corinthian Yacht Club and canceled earlier instructions to put his ketch in water. Then Lev Kowalski came in, short and bulky with bright, inquisitive eyes, spread his files on Peter's desk, and without preliminaries began, in Russian, his all-day briefing.

After Kowalski departed, Peter took the dust cover from Miss Armistead's typewriter and typed a letter in Spanish to Professor Sainz, expressing the hope that despite other commitments Sainz would be able to see him after he arrived in Madrid.

Confidential Accounts had deposited operational funds with his Washington bank, and Peter had requested their transfer to Chase Manhattan's Madrid office. Funding and the introduction to Professor Sainz were taken care of, Miss Armistead had booked him on TWA to Madrid, and TWA in turn was reserving a room at the Palace Hotel, where he would stay until he could find a small furnished apartment.

As for the agency schedule, what remained was establishing routine and emergency commo systems and training him in their use at a safe site near Bethesda. That phase began in the morning, and Peter planned to use any remaining time in reviewing the histories of the Spanish Communist party, the Royalist Movement, and the intricacies of monarchical interrelationships in Spain.

He gathered together the sheaf of notes he had made during Kowalski's briefing, put them in his attaché case, locked the office, and went down to the street. He felt tired in body and mind, so he turned the Alfa-Romeo south and went to the University Club for a swim and massage before dinner. Then he drove to his house, mixed a Canadian Club highball, fed Albéniz' *Iberia* suite into his tape recorder, and settled down in his library to read.

At ten Danny Choi came in, made a pot of coffee, and brought it to Peter, who said, "Any travel plans, Danny?"

"I've been alerted for a SEATO conference in Bangkok, but it's not firm. How long will you be away?"

"It's hard to say. At least a month; perhaps as much as six. If you've got a friend who wants to save rent, he can live here while I'm away."

Danny grinned. "All my friends want to save money, Peter. Thanks to you, I don't have that problem."

"Thanks to you I'm here instead of in a shallow grave above the Thirty-eighth Parallel," Peter reminded him. "And use up my concert tickets, Danny. Or when you're busy, Miss Armistead might like to go."

"Sure thing." He refilled Peter's cup and carried the pot out to the kitchen. Peter changed the recorder tape to one with the guitars of Montoya and Bola Sete, went back to his studies, and turned in at eleven.

On the day Peter left he received a response from Professor Sainz, saying he would be honored to help a former student of Carberry's in any way he could. He included his home address and telephone number, and expressed the hope that they would see each other in the near future.

From National Airport Peter took an Eastern flight to Kennedy International, arriving in time to check with TWA and have a light dinner before Flight 906 was called. His seat was forward in the first-class compartment, Peter having paid the amount over government-allowed economy class from his own pocket. The difference made a tax-deductible business expense.

Over the dark Atlantic stewards and stewardesses plied him with fine viands, wines, and liquors until he groggily turned off the overhead light and fell into a deep sleep. A steward wakened him to daylight, and when Peter looked out of the window he saw the Alagón River winding through the plains of Cáceres province below. Advancing his watch to seven thirty, he shaved, washed, and breakfasted on hot cakes and sausage before the big Boeing landed outside Madrid promptly at nine.

During customs inspection at Barajas Airport, the inspector expressed interest in Peter's Polaroid camera, but when Peter spoke with him in Spanish the inspector waved him amiably on. From Barajas he took a taxi into the heart of Madrid by way of Avenida América and the Paseo de la Castellana, past the graceful Cibeles Fountain to the entrance of the Palace Hotel. There he registered, left his passport with the clerk, and was shown to a fourth-floor room. From the window he could see across San Jerónimo and the plaza to the brownstone palace where the Spanish legislature met. The Prado museum with its matchless displays of Goya, El Greco, Velázquez, and Rubens was only a few blocks away.

The Castellana Hilton would be filled with Hollywood and New York types, the Ritz with British and tourists and Madrid-based diplomats, whereas the Palace and its excellent marble bar catered to a cosmopolitan clientele that included Argentines, Canadians, Indians, and Portuguese, none of whom clanged money around and roared for service. Peter viewed the Palace as one of the remaining hostels of quality in a world run mediocrity-mad. In its time, however, the Palace had housed a weird congeries of Russian aviators and tank officers, Hungarian artillerymen and Polish ordnance experts—the Communist military elite of the Republican side, all wearing civilian clothes to conceal their presence and their purpose. Stashevsky and Rosenberg had lodged there, along with Orlov, Krivitsky, and Ehrenburg. Seldom in those days had Spanish voices been heard.

From his breast pocket Peter drew a pair of horn-rimmed glasses with plain glass lenses. He fitted them on and looked at himself in the mirror. Operational Disguise had provided them for him on the grounds that spectacles were natural equipment for a scholar of Peter's ostensible seriousness. He got his watch chain from his stud box, straightened the Phi Beta Kappa key, wound the heavy gold watch that had been his father's, and hung the chain across his vest. The overall effect, he decided, resembled the assistant headmaster of a small but reasonably good preparatory school.

That much accomplished, he went to the writing table and wrote an arrival confirmation on airmail stationery, addressing the envelope to Ralph Monocacy, Box 221, Bala Cynwyd, Pennsylvania.

As far as he knew the addressee was notional, simply a drop box that served as the Headquarters end of his S/W link. The test letter contained no secret writing, but it implicitly informed Jim Hopwood that he was in Madrid, and told the S/W technicians how long his routine communications would be in transit.

There was a knock on his door. He called "Come in," and saw a chambermaid enter, arms laden with towels and fresh linen. *"Perdón, señor,"* she said politely, and bustled into the bathroom.

When she was gone, Peter removed the leather case from his Polaroid and opened the back. He pressed a concealed button, and the cartridge began to turn. Next he got out a light meter whose circular lanyard opened into a cord with a small jack at the trailing end. Plugging the jack into the cable release at the camera's edge, he thumbed the starter button and began to speak into the light meter. After a time he stopped the reel's rotation, rewound it, and when he held the "light meter" to his ear, his voice repeated the words he had spoken. The unit was a sub-miniaturized recorder, and the meter held not a photoelectric cell but a small and efficient microphone. The test over, he reassembled the camera and drew a small address book from inside his coat pocket. Many of the addresses were real; others contained his radio skeds and call signs among their numbers and letters. Optimum propagation for the Atlantic area that night was after 2200, if he chose to transmit a test message to Langley.

He left the room and went down to the desk, where he mailed the test letter, exchanged traveler's checks for pesetas, and deposited the camera, light meter, and flash unit in a strong box. From there he went outside and saw that it was a fine clear day. Chestnuts and poplars were in bud, and to the northwest the snow-covered Guadarrama ring thrust starkly toward the thin blue sky. Even this late in the spring, he reflected, the ski lift at Navacerrada Pass should be in operation.

A taxi took him to a car rental agency at Velázquez 36. Before he entered, he glanced up the block and saw a building on the opposite side—an old palace—numbered 63. During the Civil War it had headquartered the International Brigades and their commissars, André Marty and Luigi Longo. The war was more than a quarter of a century in the past, but its scars and symbols remained like perdurable lichen on a granite tomb. And the names of foreign participants on the Republican side, still living or dead, formed a roster of the Comintern's immortals: Thorez, Tito, Rajk, Nenni, Gerö, Vidali, Ulbricht, Codovilla, Stern, Pollitt,

Nelson, Swierczewski (Hemingway's "General Golz"), Durán, Gottwald. . . . Their number was endless. The unproletarian headquarters of Generals Konev, Berzin, Malinovsky, and Rokossovsky had been at Gaylord's on the Retiro. University City had been destroyed as had been the Alcázar; bullet marks remained to be seen on the Alcalá Arch. Annually the Falange honored the grave of Calvo Sotelo in East Cemetery, where assault guards had dumped his body, two bullet holes, Cheka-style, in the back of his head. His assassination had been the tocsin of rebellion.

To live in Madrid, Peter reflected, was like living on the field of Gettysburg with its somber and omnipresent memorials, the shell fragments and spent gray bullets that appeared at the turn of a spade.

Entering the agency, Peter selected a Mercedes coupe from the available cars, produced his international license, and paid the required deposit. While the agent made out papers Peter telephoned the home of Professor Sainz and was answered by a woman's voice. He said in Spanish, "Professor Sainz, please."

"Who calls him?"

"My name is Ward."

"The North American who wrote the professor?"

"The same."

"Welcome to Madrid, Sr. Ward."

"Thank you."

"A moment, while I inform the professor."

As he waited, the agent looked up and said, "Professor Eduardo Sainz?"

Peter nodded.

"Es un viejo notable," the agent said. "A remarkable old man. Do you know him?"

"We've never met."

"He is a Royalist to the death, and the archives have been his entire existence." Stamping the documents, he handed them to Peter. "With the return of the Count of Prados," he said, "our cause has been given new life, new hope. May I inquire if you see him on Royalist affairs?"

Peter adjusted his glasses. "Legal research," he said, and pocketed the car papers. Through the receiver the woman spoke again. "The professor will be delighted to receive you now and wonders if you could remain for lunch?"

"With much pleasure," Peter said. "I should be there in fifteen or twenty minutes."

A mechanic drove the Mercedes from the garage to the street. Peter got behind the wheel, consulted a map, and turned west onto Calle Sanjurjo, named in honor of the "Lion of the Riff." Passing the Isabel II Reservoir, Peter proceeded on toward the Ciudad Universitaria, turning south finally onto Calle Eslava. In the distance he could see the Hospital Clínico, which had been the scene of so many murders, so much horror and suffering, a quarter of a century before.

The home of Professor Eduardo Sainz was a modest old brownstone whose door bore a brass plate with his name, and below it the inscription: *Archivos del Movimiento Real.*

Peter drew out the antique bellpull and heard its gong echo inside the house. After a time the door was opened by a maid in starched uniform to whom Peter gave his name as he entered.

She left him in a dimly lighted hallway lined with oil paintings depicting grandees and battles of the Peninsular War. He took off his raincoat and glanced into the dark sitting room. Ancient battle flags were arrayed above and on either side of the empty fireplace, some of them tattered and stained. Corner stands held fanions and gonfalons, their motionless streamers torn and gray. Near one window a glassed wall plaque displayed a worn blue beret that Peter identified as a Royalist *boina.*

The maid returned and led him down the corridor to a high-ceilinged study whose windows overlooked a garden fallen into decay. The walls of the study were lined with bookshelves; furniture held boxes of papers piled high in apparent disorder. In front of the windows stretched a broad carved table whose cartons of books and papers framed the face of an old and white-haired man.

"Professor Sainz?" Peter said. "I'm Peter Ward."

Rising slowly, the old man shuffled out from behind the desk and extended one frail hand. "So good of you to come," his voice quavered. *"Mi casa está a su apreciable disposición."*

Before Peter could complement the formula, Sainz turned and gestured at the encircling bookcases. "My life's work," he murmured. "So little done and still so much to do. Like Ay of the Eighteenth Dynasty I have been, I suppose, the keeper of my monarch's flame." His thin face seemed to glow, and as his hand lowered it paused to finger a wispy white goatee.

"For one who dedicates himself to a cause," Peter said politely, "nothing else can be said to matter."

Sainz inclined his head in agreement. "And how did you leave our colleague Carberry?"

"In good health, I believe."

"You did not see him?"

"Regrettably, not in more than a decade," Peter admitted. "Fourteen or fifteen years."

"In his way he is a genius, that one," said Sainz with a nod. "And like yourself, Señor Profesor, a legendary figure to those who know and understand his work."

For a moment Sainz stood motionless, as though absorbed in thought. Then he said, "Will you take coffee, Dr.* Ward? Tea? A glass of *manzanilla*?"

Peter drew his watch from a vest pocket and opened the engraved cover. *"Manzanilla, por favor,"* he said, and returned the watch to his pocket.

The professor smiled faintly. "I perceive that you possess precise habits, Señor Doctor. Lamentably, as I age, I find my life increasingly disordered." Pulling a wall rope, he summoned the maid and asked that *manzanilla* be brought. It came in a silver decanter that bore the escutcheon of Castile, and when they had toasted each other Peter regretted not having learned the label of the light, sherrylike wine. The aperitif seemed to stimulate his host, who launched into an appraisal of post-Civil War Spanish politics, ending with a declaration that Generalissimo Franco was the Octavius of Spain.

"In what sense?" Peter inquired.

"He survived all the others, Dr. Ward—the plotters and intriguers, the *señoritos* and the incompetent generals, just as Octavius survived to rule." Then, somewhat to Peter's surprise, Sainz said, "I have no quarrel with Franco, the man—and I saw him often during the Crusade. But we Royalists feel that after fighting beside his Nationalists, we deserved a certain recognition, none of which has ever been forthcoming. Certainly, in 1939, Spain was in no condition to accept another king. But now—" His hands spread, veined and brittle as dry leaves. "Now, with Spain undergoing an economic renaissance, we believe the time has come to resolve the political question."

"By popular referendum?"

Sainz moved his head slowly. "The franchise in Spain—when exercised—has proved nothing unless it be that Spaniards have no capacity for democratic or republican government. Class divisions still exist, Dr. Ward, and I would ask you to bear in mind that your own revolution was anticolonial in character, not fought on class lines as was the French."

Peter lifted his glass and sipped the dry, lemon-colored wine.

Gazing at him, Sainz said in a vibrant voice, "To secure the peace and well-being of Spain, the Caudillo should step

* In Hispanic countries, law graduates are generally addressed as "Doctor."

aside now and permit the Regency Council to name to the throne not the Prince of Asturias but the legitimate heir." He lifted his glass. "Don Jaime Rodrigo Pérez y Vals Salvat, Conde de Prados. Brought back by a benign God from the purgatory of Russia—restored to us his followers at this crucial moment in the long history of Catholic Spain to assume his rightful and long-denied place on the throne." Eyes shining, he drained his glass, and as his burst of emotion subsided Peter said, "The count is well, Professor Sainz?"

"He arrived in poor health and much distracted. The last several weeks he passed in seclusion, but tomorrow," he said proudly, "it is my high privilege to be granted an audience with my monarch. Think of it, Señor Doctor, after all these years—these long, hopeless years when we believed him dead in some Russian grave!"

"It seems miraculous," Peter agreed. "And his daughter, the *condesa*?"

"Marisa is transported with joy. I, who was a childless widower, made but a poor father for the child, but"—he spread his hands again—"thanks to God they are together at last."

"She never knew her father?"

Sainz shook his head. "Her mother bore her after Don Rodrigo left with the Blue Division. That was—let me see—the late summer of nineteen forty-one."

"Why did the count go?"

"He felt a quixotic sense of obligation to fight alongside the Germans who had helped our cause, though I attempted to persuade him that Hitler had long since been reimbursed—with Spanish coal, iron, wood, and our other riches. Richly paid. Still, Rodrigo would go. He was a young man, you see, a colonel only two years before, and perhaps the difficulties of reconstructing Spain held no appeal for him. Impetuosity, I suppose." The old man sat back in his chair and stared up at the high ceiling. "He should have remained among us. We had nothing in common with the Fascists, nothing, yet he went away. First to Grafenwöhr in Bavaria for training, then in late August to Grodno. From there they marched—marched, I say—to Vitebsk and Novgorod." One hand lifted tiredly to his eyes. "At Novgorod many prisoners were taken; among them, we heard, Don Rodrigo. Through the International Red Cross we sent parcels of food and clothing, and for a time his signature was returned to us on receipts; then we heard nothing until"—his voice wavered—"a report, then another, and others still, all saying that he was dead." The old man drew himself erect. "That Don Rodrigo had died of maltreatment in Novostroika, the hell camp on the Biela River."

"Who made these reports?"

"Returned soldiers of the Blue Division, escaped prisoners, Russians who had fled the camps." He shrugged. "Many reports of his death and none of his survival. How else could we judge his fate?"

The maid entered and told the professor that he was wanted on the telephone. Excusing himself, Sainz shuffled around his desk and disappeared behind the barricade of papers and cartons while he plugged in the silenced telephone and answered.

Peter refilled their glasses and waited, hearing the old man chatter excitedly. Finally he banged down the telephone and rounded his desk, rubbing his hands ecstatically. "Marisa!" he exclaimed. "Marisa, to tell me that her father—her blood father—will see me in the morning at ten." Drawing a large handkerchief from his pocket, he wiped perspiration from his forehead. "So many years," he murmured in a remote voice. "So many, many years."

Then he seemed to recall his visitor and took his chair once more. "You must forgive me, Señor Doctor, but I—I am nearly overcome."

"I understand."

"The condition of the count—mentally far more than physically—precluded an earlier meeting. But now, *gracias a Dios*, he is able to receive me."

Peter nodded. "Then I won't expect to see you tomorrow."

"No, not tomorrow. Not tomorrow." He blinked at the light, breathed deeply, and exhaled. "Forgive me, also, for taking up your time with matters which can hold no interest for you. To spare you further, before you leave I will give you my study entitled *Problems of the Royal Movement*, which will establish—should you care to read it—the legitimacy of our claim."

"I'd be most interested."

Professor Sainz inclined his head in acknowledgment. "Now, your principal objective is perhaps a comparison of the legal bases of monarchies past and present. This subject is—by happy coincidence—one on which I lecture at the faculty of law in our university hard by. Let me cover the continent from west to east, beginning with the ascendancy and reign of the Plantagenets in the year of Our Lord eleven hundred and fifty-four, seven years after the start of the Second Crusade to recover the Holy Land."

FOUR

The professor was master of his subject, Peter conceded wearily as they rose from a long lunch that had begun at something after two, and it was apparent that the old man was fully intending to cover the entire course. So far, he had dissected the Plantagenets, the Houses of York and Stuart, with the Houses of Hanover and Windsor still remaining. The monarchies of only one country, Perfidious Albion, and another fourteen or fifteen countries ahead.

For Spain, their meal had been a frugal one: translucent slices of *jamón serrano*—ham laid in mountain snow and cured by the slow winter sun—fresh figs, and *cocido*, a dish of yellow chick-peas—*Cicer arietinum*, the professor supplied—cooked and steamed with bits of beef, chicken, and bacon. As they walked back to the professor's library-office, he explained that although his medical regimen did not allow coffee, he hoped that Peter would partake.

Peter accepted gladly, hoping it would help him stay awake, and when the maid served him from a heavy silver pot, she left a tray of *turrones* on the table beside his cup. Peter offered the sweets to Sainz, but the older man declined, saying his teeth could not hazard the contest. And so as Peter gulped down the first demitasse of heavily silted coffee, the professor resumed his lecture with the accession of the first of the Hanoverian kings, George I, in 1714.

Drowsily, Peter heard Sainz drone on about Walpole and the South Sea Bubble, and as his heavy eyes began to close the front door opened and running feet neared the library door.

Through it burst a figure in a beautifully tailored hand-woven-tweed walking suit. Without even a glance at Peter she halted before Sainz and spoke rapidly and excitedly—so rapidly, Peter thought at first, as to make her Spanish unintelligible. Then he heard soft slurring syllables that reminded him of Portuguese or Piedmontese Italian, and while he was weighing the two, Professor Sainz interrupted his caller in Spanish. With a nod in Peter's direction he said chidingly, "Marisa, my daughter, we have a guest. Dr. Peter Ward of the United States."

Peter rose as she turned to face him.

Sainz said, "Dr. Ward is a colleague, Marisa, and the

former student of a very old friend and colleague. Doctor, the Condesa de Prados."

She was of medium height, fine-boned, and her youthful figure was erect without artificial rigidity. The dimensions of her bosom were modest under the tweed, though Peter suspected her bust was under considerable restraint. Her face was oval and boyish, and the parted lips of her uncompromising mouth revealed straight white teeth. Her nose was small and even, the nostrils equine, and the conformation of her dark brown eyes was so close to almond that they reminded him abruptly of his dead wife. Above them her eyebrows curved like delicate *krises*, accented by the light olive of her skin. The chin was small and stubborn, and her ears were hidden by a bouffant styling of hair so darkly brown as to be nearly black.

Her head tilted as she moved smoothly toward him. "Dr. Ward," she said in the patrician accents of an English boardingschool pupil.

"Condesa." Peter lifted her hand and bent over it momentarily, then stepped back.

Sainz said, "We were speaking Catalan, Doctor. Marisa, pray continue in Castilian."

Her eyes left Peter lingeringly and she walked with feral grace to a chair beside the old man. "I doubt that our . . . intrigues . . . will interest Dr. Ward."

"On the contrary," Sainz said reprovingly. "He is interested in all monarchical matters. To be in this room today is to witness yet another advance toward our goal—the throne of Spain for the House of Prados."

Her mouth set, and as her eyes returned to the professor, Peter saw her in profile and realized how completely mistaken had been his speculative vision of her. María Luisa Pérez y Vals Delgado was no desiccated zealot, no mannish Joan of Arc, but a strikingly beautiful young woman of evident intelligence, controlled grace, and implicit pride.

"I was saying," she said in lilting Spanish, "that Don Felipe has persuaded Paco to summon the Brigadas for review by my father."

"And you are opposed, my daughter?"

"Unalterably opposed."

Turning to Peter, Professor Sainz said, "Don Felipe Carbajal is the philosophical leader of our Movement—our *impulsor*. Paco is Coronel Francisco Arastegui, military commander of the Brigadas."

"Don Eduardo," Marisa said tightly, "what is your opinion?"

"My opinion?" The old man shrugged. "I am an archivist,

a keeper of relics, a memorializer of the past. The direction of the Movement is not in my hands."

"But if it were," she persisted, "what would your counsel be?"

"I would be better prepared to form an opinion were you to ask me tomorrow—after my interview with the count."

"My father's health, his appearance, have nothing to do with it," she said; then, with a glance of near appeal at Peter, "My reasons are: first, the timing is ill-advised. So far our Movement has suffered no repressions, no sanctions by the government. Permitting the count to review our forces so soon after his return would perhaps persuade the government that we represented a threat to its existence. Second, we have been able to organize and spread our influence for the very reason that we were ignored by the government, not persecuted as, for example, the unfortunate signers of the inter-European declaration. I say that demonstrations now in favor of my father—particularly any that might be construed as politically significant—are premature, entirely premature. Our efforts should continue as in the past, on an individual rather than a public, a mass, basis. We must not appear to be appealing to the people over the heads of the government. Franco would never tolerate it, and we require his tolerance to gain our ends."

Sainz ran the flat of one thumbnail slowly across his goatee. "Will Paco follow your—the count's—wishes in the matter?"

"I suppose he will," she sighed, and laced her tapering fingers together, lowering them into her lap. "But Paco is a lover of spectacles, of dust rising from the boots of marching men. His position is that the Brigadas deserve the opportunity to assert their loyalty to my father—now. That is what he says, yet I am not convinced that he believes it. Please side with me, my uncle."

Sainz appeared to be absorbed in deep thought. With a vague nod he turned to Peter and said, "Our country is not accustomed to the techniques of political communication, Doctor. Yours is. May I solicit your opinion?"

"I would be most reluctant to give it."

Marisa gave a derisive laugh. "The American position—equivocal as always." To the professor she said, "Counsel them to abandon the project for now—delay it at least until the time of the next scheduled review."

Sainz sighed heavily. "Very well, Marisa, since it is so important to you."

Her features relaxed and she smiled. "Only because it is important to me?"

"Because I esteem your judgment so highly."

"I prefer the codicil," she said gently, and rose. "Dr. Ward, I wish you success in your work."

"Thank you," Peter said as he got to his feet. "With your father restored to you—and you to him—I wish you both every happiness."

Bending over, she kissed the old man's forehead, gave her hand to Peter, and walked lithely from the room. *Sol y sombra,* he thought. Sun and shadow—the moods of Spain.

Still gazing at the doorway, Sainz said, "María Luisa was named after the queen of Carlos IV and her education has been to fit her to rule: she speaks—in addition to Castilian and Catalan—Galician, French, English, Italian, German, and Russian. At the university she was an apt student of political science, and last year I had the signal honor of awarding her a doctorate in law."

"Even outside Spain those accomplishments are rare for a woman."

"She has an excellent mind, Doctor, and as our *infanta* will be of monumental help to the count, her father."

Peter said, "I've imposed upon you too long already, Señor Profesor, and you have other affairs to attend to."

"No, no. One or two telephone calls, and I will be free to continue."

Drawing out his watch, Peter looked at it and put it back. "In any case this is *siesta* time, and as a visitor I feel obligated to honor Spanish custom. You've been most liberal with your time, and I appreciate it greatly."

Slowly Sainz rose. "Tomorrow, as you know, I will be occupied. You will return the following day?"

"If it is to your convenience."

"Entirely." Sainz pulled the bell cord, and before the maid appeared he said, "You took note of a certain . . . hostility on Marisa's part toward your country?"

"Yes."

"As yet she has not decided whether America is Machiavellian, stupid, or merely uninformed. Nor is she able to rationalize the wartime partnership of the United States and Russia—the country that captured and tortured her father."

"In that she is not alone."

"Also, she feels that American indecision, or at least inaction, is responsible for many of the world's ills: the partition of Germany, the Berlin Wall, the communization of Cuba, and the presence there of two Spanish-born agents of death—the so-called generals Lister and Bayo, notorious for their bloody roles in our civil conflict."

Hearing the maid's footsteps, Peter merely nodded. "Again let me thank you for your hospitality, Señor Profesor. *Hasta pasado mañana.*"

"De nada. Y que le vaya bien, Dr. Ward."

Peter followed the maid down the long corridor, thanked her, and left the house. As he got into his car he turned and looked back at the depository of Royalist relics, history, and hopes, thinking of the wise and loyal old man whose apocalyptic vision had made him their guardian, and of the young woman, still little more than a girl, who was so integral to the plans and preparations of the Royalist Movement.

Driving down Calle Eslava, he reflected on the ease with which he had penetrated the first barrier that separated him from the Conde de Prados, and decided that in time he might be able to count upon Sainz as an unwitting ally.

Tomorrow marked the first meeting between the old professor and the count whom he had not seen in more than a quarter of a century. Surely Sainz would comment the following day if he were in any way uneasy over the authenticity of the royal returnee. Never having known her father, Marisa was not a reliable witness, though photographs of him—even paintings—must be available to her and to Sainz for comparison. The count's former friends and comrades-in-arms would quickly detect any false notes and denounce the imposture. Still, Peter mused, a quarter of a century in Siberia could radically alter the physique and appearance of any man, damage his mind, destroy his powers of recall. . . .

Reaching Avenida José Antonio, the Gran Vía, he drove past the Hotel Florida, where Hemingway had written his one play while the hotel was under bombardment. He noticed the baroque and neoclassic buildings with their fashionable shops and cafés, the moving crowds of well-dressed, affluent-looking *madrileños,* and thought that had a substantial middle class existed as a buffer between Spain's social and political extremes the Civil War might never have been fought.

The Palace doorman took over his Mercedes. When Peter applied at the desk for his room key, the clerk coughed nervously, and Peter became aware of a man rising from a chair and approaching him from an oblique angle. Turning, he faced the man and waited until he spoke.

"Pardon, you are Señor Ward?" he inquired politely.

"Yes."

"I am from the National Security and I—"

"Sorry, but I've already made banking arrangements." Peter pocketed his key and began moving around the man.

Coloring, the man stepped closer to Peter. "The Dirección de Seguridad Nacional is not a bank, *señor.* It is like—how shall I say?—your FBI."

"Good God! Have I done something wrong?" Peter's jaw dropped. "Are you going to arrest me?"

"That depends, *señor*. You may answer my questions in your room or, if you prefer, our headquarters is but a short walk away."

Peter turned slowly to the clerk. "This gentleman claims he's from your FBI. Is he?"

The clerk swallowed. Embarrassed by complicity, he said, "I am afraid it is so."

"He wants to ask me some questions. We can go to my room or to wherever his shop is located. I'd just as soon it was here. Tell me"—he leaned on the counter—"is it *safe* to go to my room with him?"

The clerk's face was stricken. Eyes fixed on the agent's, he blurted, "Yes—yes, of course it is."

Turning back to the agent, Peter said, "You got an ID card, or anything to prove you're okay?"

Patiently the agent drew out his billfold and produced a plastic-clad identity card. Peter took it from him, studied the yellowed photograph, then the agent's face. "I can't read Spanish, but I guess it's okay. That picture must have been taken a long time ago, eh?" One corner of the card was covered by a ribbon in gold and scarlet, the national colors. He returned it to the agent and beckoned to the clerk. In a hoarse whisper he said, "Confidentially, friend, what's the rap?"

The clerk's face paled. "The—the *rap*?" His mouth clamped shut and he scuttled away.

The agent tapped Peter's arm. "Are you satisfied now, *señor?*"

"I guess so," Peter said resignedly. He squared his shoulders and led the agent to the nearest elevator. Unlocking his room door, he said, "Make yourself at home, *señor*. We got lots better than this in the States, but for a foreign country it'll do."

The agent drew himself erect. "This hotel is one of Spain's finest. It is one of the finest in the world."

Peter eyed him. "You seen much of the world?" Easing into a chair, he saw the agent's mouth open to retort, then snap shut. "Okay," Peter said. "Shoot."

"Shoot?"

"Your questions," Peter said impatiently. "Come on, ask your questions."

The agent wet his lips. He cleared his throat and attempted a hard stare. "Why do you come to Spain?"

"You read English? Read this." Peter got up, opened one of his bags, and drew out an envelope that contained an engraved certificate from the Blackstone Foundation describing the purposes of Peter's grant. When the agent had scanned it, he returned it to Peter. "This document could be forged."

"Anything can be forged," Peter said dryly. "Why the hell would anyone bother to forge a thing like this?"

"To give you a reason for being here, a reason to explain your contacts while you carry out your real work."

"My *real* work? You calling me a liar?" He towered over the agent, who stepped back and whipped a sheet of paper from his pocket.

"Could *this* be your real work, *señor?*" Unfolding it, he showed Peter a closely typed mimeographed page. "This subversive document?"

Peter held it toward the window, studied the captions, and returned it to the agent. Shaking his head, he said, "You'll have to tell me what it says."

With mounting exasperation the Spaniard roared, "It is a document from the Communist party of Spain!"

Peter blinked. "Communists in Spain? I thought you fellows had cleaned house."

"The Communist party of Spain in exile!" the agent shouted.

"Where?"

"What do you mean, 'where'?"

"I mean where's the exile?"

"We don't know—this could come from Paris, or Moscow, or Argentina."

"Must be a lot of exiles," Peter said calmly, and tapped the quivering sheet with a fingernail. "What's so important about it?"

"It is a declaration against the Chief of State." The agent's face was tomato red.

"That's not neighborly," Peter remarked. He took off his glasses and began to polish them. "What's it got to do with me?"

"What it has to do with you is that it was found here, *señor*—here in this room."

"Where?"

"There—over there." The agent strode to the writing table and pointed to a spot on the carpet near the wall.

Peter sighed loudly. "Good Lord, I saw something there when I moved in this morning—that must be it. I guess the maid didn't clean the room so good after the last customer." He smiled cheerfully at the agent, as though unaware that he had led him into unintended revelation.

The agent realized it, however; he wiped his forehead and stared at the incriminating sheet. "You saw it there when you occupied the room?" he said unhappily.

"That's what I said, friend. Guess that clears everything up, doesn't it?" He patted the agent's back. "Russians here in my room, eh? Someone made a mistake. A very bad mistake."

"Yes," the agent said dully, "a very bad mistake was made."

Peter moved his head sympathetically. "Uh—who was it found that document and reported it?"

"The room maid," the agent said helplessly.

"Then I guess the management better look into just how well these rooms are cleaned up, eh? The criminal probably checked out just before I got here."

The agent nodded wordlessly.

In a kindly voice Peter said, "Much ado about nothing, I'd say. Our old neighbor, L.B.J., gets criticized every day, but don't give it no mind. He—"

"L.B.J.?" the agent gasped "Your *neighbor*?"

"Why, back in Texas he's just folks—same as the rest of us. 'Course he's in Washington right now, but one day he'll be back in Blanco County, and we'll all—"

Hastily, the agent stuffed the Communist flier into one pocket and gave an agonized glance at the door.

"Leaving?" Peter asked interestedly. "If you got time I could order up some drinks while you tell me about this Communist business. There's lots about it I don't understand, but you being a professional on the subject—"

"Perhaps some other time," the agent said with a forced smile. "Please pardon this unfortunate mistake, *señor*. Believe me, it is most regrettable."

Peter waved one hand. "No trouble, no trouble," he said genially. "If a man didn't make mistakes I say he wouldn't be human. Right?"

"Right!" the agent said fervently, shook hands with Peter, and retreated to the doorway. Whirling, he unbolted the door and fled. Peter's smile faded and his eyes narrowed. After a moment he went into the bathroom, ran bath water, and dumped the unused towels into the tub. When they were drenched he turned off the water and rang for the room maid. He filled his pipe, lighted it, and heard a knock on his door.

"*¿Señor?*"

"Come in."

The door opened and the maid entered, the same maid who had brought in linen earlier that day. She was beyond middle age, and strands of white were threaded through the long black hair that showed below her lacy service cap.

"Towels," he said, and gestured toward the bathroom.

As the maid began walking toward it, he fell in behind her and gestured at the sodden mass in the tub. She bent over the side of the tub and Peter shut the bathroom door.

At the click of the lock she looked around and her face froze. *"¿Qué?"* she said hoarsely. *"¿Qué pasa, señor?"*

"How long have you worked here?" Peter said; then, in Spanish, *"¿Por cuanto tiempo has trabajado aquí?"*

"¿Aquí—en este hotel?" she faltered.

"Exacto."

"Dos—dos años. Dos años y medio."

Two—two and a half years, Peter translated. He said in Spanish: "I think that's long enough, don't you? I think you ought to give notice about now and depart for the country. Very likely you have a sick uncle who could benefit from your prolonged care."

She drew herself upright, hands closing into fists. "Why—why should I do that?"

"Because the trick didn't work," Peter snapped. "The phony party communiqué. If I see you tomorrow, *señora,* you'll have DSN agents crawling over you like flies."

Slowly, stiffly, she walked toward him, and Peter saw her cold, bitter eyes. The eyes of a fanatic, he told himself, of a La Pasionaria, a Federica Montseny. She had the hands and build of a peasant woman, a barricade fighter, a *miliciana.* As she reached for the doorknob Peter grated, "Towels. Dry ones."

Robotlike, she went back to the tub, gathered the dripping bundle into her arms, and passed Peter unseeingly. He took his pipe from his mouth, glanced at it, and lighted the tobacco again. The hall door opened and closed.

Like rats in the woodwork, he mused as he went slowly back to the bedroom.

The attempt to compromise him with the Spanish Service had not originated with the room maid; she was no more than a low-level agent of the *konspiratsia,* well removed from any center of importance. The effort had failed, but it gave clear evidence that his presence in Madrid was known and was of significance to someone—the KGB *rezidentura,* the clandestine directorate of the Spanish Communist party, Cuban agents . . . possibly some anti-Royalist group.

The episode, in any case, was a poor omen, a sign to be remembered. Its immediate effect was to remind him of the dangers that surrounded a lone agent operating in a foreign milieu against an entrenched and alert opposition.

Laying aside his pipe, he picked up the telephone and began calling rental agencies for a quiet, secure apartment.

Part II

From the wide, trefoil-arched window he peered through

gathering dusk at the garden below, at the tiled walks and carefully tended shrubbery, the close-nipped plots of grass, and the tall trees arranged so as to shelter the enclave from sun and driving rain.

Now, in the spring, the branches were laden with buds, the green promises of life, and warmly healing air—the miracle of seasonal rebirth that passed so briefly above the Arctic Circle as to be forgotten in the muffled quiet of winter.

What light there was in the cavernous room entered by the window, and it was enough to show his shadowed profile, the trenchlike scar carved deeply along the right side of his face.

His head moved and his gaze slowly shifted beyond the distant garden wall to the cathedral of Nuestra Señora de la Almudena with its twin spires, and beyond, the Royal Palace barely visible in the fading light. He remembered vaguely the vast gardens of El Moro Park with its towering acacias, and the vendors of sweets and flavored ices along the labyrinthine paths. Other memories gathered at the gates of his mind, murmured briefly for entrance, and were denied. In time, he promised himself, everything would fit into place, become clear and properly defined.

He was sitting in a richly brocaded chair that was part of the furnishings of the oak-paneled library in the hereditary town residence of the Prados family. The setting was remotely familiar, as though it formed the substance of an ancient, dimly remembered dream or its description had been given him by voices from long ago. He knew that the petit palace had been built early enough to have been despoiled when Murat entered Madrid, sacked after the insurrection broke out, and shell-damaged during the long defense of Madrid. It held no warmth for him, no reassuring childhood memories to flesh his skeletal past. It symbolized in some way the pervasive strength of an aristocracy to which he was again allied, rather than the comfort and security of a home.

His face lowered and his eyes settled on the hands that rested quietly in his lap. Dully he gazed at their callused flesh striated with old white scars. Then, with a covert glance at the oaken door, he reached beneath his belt and drew out, slowly and craftily, the treasure that had helped him survive. Worn thin and battered, the tin spoon lay in the palm of his hand like a jewel of great price. He had obtained it so long ago that he was uncertain how ownership had been achieved. Had he bargained bread for it with some short-term prisoner? Was it bought from a guard with rubles earned with his blood? Stolen from a blatnyak *in one of the periodic battles? Taken from an ice-clad corpse in the Vorkuta forest?*

Or had he gained it on the battlefield by plundering some German, Russian, or Spanish body?

However it had come into his possession he had cherished it as a priest a crucifix, and it had become an instrument of salvation.

His hands molded its dull outlines with the pride of secret possession as his mind resolved again that he would never let it be separated from him, either in this life or another.

With care he returned his treasure to its place of concealment, and as his head lifted he saw that the garden was dark now. Darkness was a friend, a companion to rest and healing, a refuge from icy wind. Empty now, his hands twitched, and some latent, recidive impulse stirred him from the chair where he had sat unmoving since nearly noon. The long oppression of time had left him insensate to its passage and substituted in its place awareness of a simpler cycle: work and non-work. Nothing more.

As he crossed the dim room the tension of his belt reminded him that he was gaining weight; at least eight kilos since the day he had boarded the train that took him from Vorkuta. They had been kind to him here, those strangers he had come so recently to know. Gentle, endlessly helpful and understanding; caring for him, answering his every wish, and asking nothing in return. They seemed, all of them, like beings from another world, some perfect planet where siblags *were unknown, whose clean pure air itself could strangle* volkovoy. *An isolated civilization oblivious of beasts outside its walls . . .*

He opened the door and walked down the corridor, seeing no one but a maid polishing candelabra in the comedor. *His steps were nearly soundless, the steps of a man conditioned to stealth in all things, and so he passed unnoticed into the pantry and thence to the cellar door.*

Quietly he descended the dark staircase, and at the bottom turned and walked until his outstretched fingers met the wall of the gardener's shed. Undoing the latch, he felt for the stand of tools, fingering each by rote until he touched the cold, sharp blade of a double-headed axe.

Lifting it to his shoulder, he felt the oaken haft slide onto the old protective callus that had formed there over the years, turned to orient himself, and saw the lighter panes of the garden door.

Outside, he moved with unaccustomed vigor toward the foot of the garden, as though his contact with the garden soil were theurgic, inducing strength from the soft, fresh earth.

The tree was there ahead, the old one he had studied from his post beside the window. Slim and tall, its branches spread six meters above his head.

He tested the blade with his thumb, hardly believing the sharpness of the well-honed edge, then smiled softly in the dark. To work with proper implements was satisfying—not the ruined salvage of some kolkhoz, *but a fine, well-balanced axe like this one: sharp, sturdy, and light.*

He swung it in a surge of strength, and the solid chuk *echoed from the garden walls. He swung again, and the long chip flew free, a bone-white gash marking the site. Spreading his legs, he struck like a Stakhanovite striving to surpass his norm, the harsh concussion of his blows resounding through the darkness until a shaft of light flared outward from the house.*

Checking the half-delivered blow, he turned and saw Marisa silhouetted in the library window, one hand lifted to her throat.

Staring.

FIVE

The apartment Peter rented was on Calle Espalter in an old graystone building halfway up the hill between the Prado Museum and the Retiro Gardens. According to the agent, the apartment was owned by a retired *procurador* and his wife who were spending the spring at Algeciras for their health.

The apartment was furnished in Renaissance-cum-Victorian elegance, with cabinets of porcelain figurines and milk glass, gilded sconces, and dull tapestries that looked so fragile as to disintegrate at a touch.

In addition to two months' rent in advance, Peter paid deposits for gas, electricity, and telephone, plus an escrow sum against breakage, and moved in with one bag before nightfall. His overt residence would continue to be the Palace Hotel; the apartment was for privacy and seclusion—a safehouse, in agency parlance.

From one window he could look down on the southmost end of the Prado; from another he was able to make out one of the neoclassic gates of the Retiro and a portion of foliage beyond.

Peter had been offered several modern apartments and had

rejected them because of their thin walls and floors, and because his neighbors were more likely to be curious about him than were the elderly folk who dwelt along Espalter. The deciding factor in his choice had not been the old concert grand, but the inclusion among the furnishings of a German radio-phonograph in a handsome walnut cabinet. Opening its doors, he scanned the all-band receiver, set it on shortwave, and heard an announcer speaking from Pretoria.

In addition to its attack on the Church and the Spanish Chief of State, the Communist party flier planted in his room contained a list of the daily schedules of Spanish-language programs over Radio España Independiente—broadcast from Moscow—on the 21, 25, and 30 meter bands. Seven and a half hours a day, if anyone cared to listen.

From Moscow, Dolores Ibarruri, La Pasionaria, could harangue in safety, no longer the inciter of crowds in the Plaza España or the Ramblas of Barcelona. Her aging voice came distantly through static, not over the barricades of Sevilla, the trenches of Badajoz. She was a pensioner of the Soviet state, secure with her once-young lover in the Valhalla of the Comintern—La Pasionaria, whose teeth, it was said, had torn out the throat of a priest.

Turning off the radio, Peter opened the wall safe and reset the combination. Then he locked his recorder-transmitter inside the circular vault, hung his clothing in a bedroom closet, and went to the window.

Evening had come over the city. Lights outlined jutting skyscrapers along the Gran Vía; the Torre de Madrid made a glowing pylon against the night.

At Langley it was midday; Hopwood and his *camarilla* would be enjoying lunch in the special dining room, while the sunlit halls flowed with cafeteria-bound personnel. At Southlands his sister and brother-in-law might be fishing for trout in the freshets of Gander Creek; Danny Choi would be devouring a sandwich at a library table, his eyes never leaving his book.

And Avery Thorne . . . Peter stretched his arms and turned from the window. Was Avery in Hong Kong, a guest of MI-5? In Bangkok, Seoul, or Saigon? Relaxing in the steam baths of Atami or the Tokyo Onsen?

A few more days and Thorne would be back at Langley. After clearing his desk he would check briefly on Seraph's progress, then turn to other things.

Lighting his pipe, Peter pulled on his raincoat and walked around the corner to a delicatessen, where he bought an evening newspaper, a bottle of Canadian Club, and two of Rioja Tinto. Back in the apartment he mixed a highball, read Spain's version of world news, and noticed in the entertainment section an announcement that the famous Calé Flamenco Troupe was performing a limited engagement at El Guante; hours: 2330, 0230, and 0400 each night.

His watch informed him that it was eight o'clock; Madrid's cocktail time—the *aperitivo*—was drawing to a close. He showered, shaved, and dressed, and took a taxi to the Balmoral Club on Hermosilla, a fashionable nontourist establishment set in a modern brick-faced building. Chauffeured foreign cars choked the narrow street, and when Peter entered the anteroom the number of poodles under the charge of a redcoated *chico* reminded him of New York's 21.

The interior was thickly carpeted, and racks of Iberian ibex hung from the paneled walls. Behind the bar was mounted a large black bird that resembled a vulture but was, in fact, a bustard. The Balmoral was one of the principal rendezvous for the jet set of Madrid, a place where Marisa, the young Condesa de Prados, and her friends might meet daily at a fixed hour and always at the same oak table.

Peter drank at the bar, admiring the handsomely dressed females with their escorts, nibbling parched corn from a bowl at his hand, and considering tentative plans for the evening.

By ten the Balmoral was nearly empty, so Peter left and taxied to Valentin's, although it was difficult to obtain dinner at a good Madrid restaurant much before eleven. There was a sparse group of early diners on the first floor, non-Spanish for the most part, and Peter requested the second floor with its red-and-white-checked tablecloths and its walls nearly covered with framed photographs of famous guests.

He began with *almejas marinara*—small steamed clams in a sauce of olive oil, garlic, and parsley; ate half a dozen oysters from Santander, and finished with a plate of *centolla* —the cold, boiled legs of Vizcayan spider crab. All this he washed down with the better part of a chilled bottle of Marqués de Riscal *blanco*.

Declining dessert, he drank two demi-*tazas* of thick black coffee, and walked three blocks through the cool night air to El Guante's lighted entrance. The walls and ceiling of its steeply slanting staircase gave out below on a series of wide-arched rooms, as though the Mozarabic setting derived from the crypts of Christian catacombs. Tables were arranged on three floor levels that resembled broad curved steps, leading down to the main floor, which ended in a raised platform. On it were seated in a half circle the flamenco troupe's supporting cast: the *jaleadores*, whose handclapping and spirited cries provided background for the *cantaores*, the singers; and the *bailaores*, the dancers, male and female. The men had on short, tight-fitting bolero jackets with white ruffled shirts; the women's eyes were kohl-rimmed and they wore heavy pancake makeup that warmed the natural olive of their skins. Their bodices were deeply décolleté, and their long, hip-clinging skirts, flounced and ruffled, flared gracefully below.

Two of the seated men were guitarists; tambourines lay beside the women's shoes; and the troupe's elder—a bald man with a Goyaesque face—silently fingered his ornately carved *gralla,* the Catalonian flageolet.

Peter's initial brandy cost over two hundred pesetas, El Guante's way of collecting both couvert and minimum, and as he warmed the glass between his hands, he glanced around at the gathering crowd and the walls decorated with highly polished copper plates and utensils that were the nightclub's only decor.

He scanned the features of the seated performers, noting the Moorish-gypsy stamp that marked the Andalusians apart from the blood heritages of the rest of Spain. The men had Semitic noses and deep-set, watchful eyes; the women narrow waists, full bosoms, white teeth, and sensuous lips.

In the eighth century the Moors had invaded Spain through the port of Cádiz in Andalucía, and to see modern-day Andalusians was to doubt that El Cid's campaign to drive them out had been effective.

A guitarist began to strum idly, the notes gathering speed, volume, and meaning until they pierced the smoke and conversation that permeated the low-ceilinged room. He was joined by the tapping of a woman's heel and toe—*zapateando,* it was called. The other guitarist answered with a rhythmic pattern, and the first of the *jaleadores* clapped his leathery palms in the sharply cracking sound unique to the flamenco.

Within moments the interplay of voice, instrument, and rhythm blended into a recognizable pattern—the *mirabrá,* sensual and picaresque—and from behind the platform's curtained side appeared a dancer in scarlet silk flamenco costume trimmed richly with black lace. Her glistening ebony hair was parted at the crown and drawn back on either side, showing only the pearl-hung lobes of her ears. Pinned above the part in her hair was a yellow gardenia, and as she turned toward the audience her heels rapped a provocative staccato.

Her body was slim, almost immature in comparison with the older women of the troupe, her makeup less exaggerated. The effect she made was one of detached innocence that contrasted with the frankly carnal faces behind her. She was young, Peter knew, no more than twenty now, it having been two years since he had met her in Barcelona when she was eighteen. She was of Andalusian-gypsy blood, her name was Francisca, and she was known as Paquí.

From the wings leaped a stick-thin male dancer with a vulpine face and hair in ringlets that covered his collar. The drumming of his *botas* drowned out the more delicate tapping of Paquí's heels, and as he neared her, posturing, spinning, and preening himself, Peter realized that however sensual their dance the androgyne did not exist in a sexual dimension.

He watched with pleasure, hearing the jangle of tambourines, the hot cries of the supporting cast. Sweat rolled down the faces of the guitarists until the dance and its accompaniment reached a thunderous crescendo. Silence filled the room, and Paquí ran from the stage, followed by her partner.

Peter joined in the applause. Then, as two of the supporting dancers arose and began the measured cadence of a *solear,* he got up and went backstage. He found Paquí's dressing room, knocked on the door, and heard her call, *"¿Quién es?"*

"Pedro."

"Pedro. ¿Que Pedro?"

Peter smiled. *"¿Hay más de un Pedro en tu vida?"*

"Ah, no—no es posible!" She flung the door open and gazed at him with wide, unbelieving eyes. *"Pedro. ¡Mi Pedro!"*

Her arms encircled his neck, and he lifted her as their lips met longingly. Lowering her, he said, "Come."

"But where? Pedro, I have another performance—"

"Not for nearly three hours."

Drawing away, she glanced around. "What—what will I tell them?"

"Say I am from American television."

She smiled. "Always you have the right answers. Very well, I will go with you—even though I know what you want with me."

"How did you know?"

Standing on tiptoe, she bit the lobe of his ear. "Because I want the same of you."

She gathered up a black mantilla and drew it around her head. Peter covered her shoulders with his raincoat, and together they left by the stage exit and walked to the street.

A taxi took them to Calle Espalter, and while she waited in the light mist Peter shouted for the *sereno,* who appeared after a while from around the corner, tipped his hat, and unlocked the apartment entrance. Peter gave him the expected two pesetas and three more, guided Paquí to the lift, and kissed her until the elevator reached his floor.

Opening his door, he drew the raincoat from her shoulders, turned on a ceiling lamp, and heard the quick intake of her breath.

"So beautiful, Pedro. Such a beautiful place to live!"

He nodded, realizing that to a gypsy girl raised in the

chalk caves of Sacromonte, any habitation with floor and ceiling would seem an Alcázar. Her tribe had lived in communal misery, displaying to tourists female children in wildly orgiastic dances, their wiry, dusty bodies writhing in simulation of an instinct they were still too undeveloped to feel.

Paquí had known her mother, but of her father's identity she had never been sure. Her beauty had saved her from a begging bowl, and her dancing skill from outright prostitution. At twenty—unless she were fortunate enough to marry outside her tribe—she would dance only another ten years before retirement to the role of handclapper and tambourinist, for the women of Andalucía were as quick to age as they were to mature.

"You have lived here long, Pedro?"

"Since late afternoon."

"Really? Then how long have you been in Spain?"

"Only since this morning."

Her dark eyebrows drew together. "How did you find me, *querido?*"

"Through the newspaper announcement."

She glanced at him doubtfully and sighed. "At least we are together. How much I have missed you these last two years. Where have you been, *mi amor?* What have you been doing?"

Lifting a bottle of Rioja, he said, "Wine or whiskey?"

"Wine—because I must dance again. But on Saturday night I can drink whiskey—and Sunday as well. All day if you wish."

"Saturday night," he repeated in half-promise. He opened the wine bottle and poured two glasses.

"Amor," she said, lifting the glass to her lips.

"Y tiempo."

They danced to music from the radio, the stiff flounces of her *faralais* rustling against him as they turned. He felt her body quiver, and when the music stopped he framed her face with his hands and joined their lips. Her body pressed against him and her breathing quickened; eyes closed, she freed one arm and unhooked the back of her scarlet dress. Drawing away, she let it slip to the floor, then undid the layered crinoline petticoat. He lifted her in his arms and carried her into the darkened bedroom where, naked beside him, she gave him her breasts, her orange-scented body, and bit his shoulder flesh until he could feel the hot, slow seepage of his blood.

At two o'clock he stirred her reluctantly from sleep, gathered her clothing from the living-room floor, and helped her dress in the near darkness of their room.

For a while they waited in the mist for a taxi, then Peter got out his Mercedes and drove Paquí back to El Guante's stage entrance. He got out of the car and bought her a fresh gardenia from an urchin, saw her partner smoking in the shadows, and kissed her a long good night. As the door closed behind her he bought an early edition of *ABC* from an old woman, then got into the Mercedes and turned on the overhead light.

Dim as it was he could scan the headlines, and from the second lead a name jumped out to shock him into sick incomprehension:

Murió un gran viejo, the story began. *El Profesor Eduardo Sainz de la Universidad Central fué atropellado brutalmente esta noche por un coche desconocido . . .*

A great old man is dead, Peter translated numbly. Professor Eduardo Sainz of the university was brutally run over this evening by an unknown car . . .

. . . *con el resultado que el Profesor Sainz dejó de vivir en el acto. . . .*

. . . as a result of which Professor Sainz died instantaneously. . . .

With an effort Peter thrust the paper aside, shoved the gear stick forward, and heard the tires squeal as the Mercedes shot ahead. When he reached Espalter he garaged the automobile, found the *sereno* to let him in, and raced up the stairs to his floor.

Opening the wall safe, he took out the recorder, activated it, and spoke into the disguised microphone.

"Seraph sending," he said in a tightly controlled voice. "This is Message Number One. Repeat: Seraph Message Number One. Sainz killed last night by hit-and-run driver. No details yet. He was to see count in morning for first time. I had brief meeting with countess at Sainz home prior his death. I plan attend funeral and develop countess as last means of access under operational plan. Advise any collateral information that might relate to Sainz's death. Finis."

Unplugging the microphone, he rewound the tape and connected the flash unit to the recorder. The flash attachment was actually a VHF transmitter that used the Heaviside effect in reaching Langley's antenna field. Peter consulted his notebook and set the transmitter on the proper frequency. Then he carried the slave units to a window, opened the casements, and pressed a red button on the flash case. From now on the sequence of events was automatic. For a few moments the transmitter emitted silent signals that activated an automatic recorder at Langley. Then from the camera case came a brief whirring sound as Peter's verbal message was compressed and transmitted as a single burst. The red button popped up and Peter closed the window. Transmission was completed; message sent.

He erased the tape, put his equipment back into the wall safe, locked it, and poured himself a short drink. The Madrid station might eventually report Sainz's death in a routine dispatch rather than by radio, since Sainz was of no operational interest to the station.

He was to me, though, Peter murmured. He pulled off his tie and slumped into a chair. As he sipped his drink he pondered the temporal relationship between Sainz's long-awaited audience with the count and his having been struck down by an unidentified car. Was there a causal link as well? Was the death of Sainz only misadventure, or had he been killed to cancel his morning audience with the Conde de Prados?

What threat did Sainz pose, if any, and to whom?

That he had been a loyal servant of the Royalist cause was indisputable. He was too old to take an active role in Royalist intrigues to enthrone the count, reluctant even to counsel Marisa when she sought his advice, so it was unlikely that internal Royalist jealousies had provoked his liquidation.

Sainz must have known the count as long or longer than anyone living—including the count's daughter. But surely Sainz was not the only man alive who had known the count well enough before his capture to be able to authenticate him now.

Or could it be that . . . ?

His brain was tired, his eyes smarted with fatigue. In the morning he would get at the problem again with a fresh and alert mind. At night fantasies flowed too easily.

Draining his glass, he turned off the lights, went into the bedroom, and slid between cool sheets that still gave off the sweet scent of orange blossoms.

SIX

Early in the morning Peter walked from his apartment to the hotel and breakfasted in the Palace grill. The meal was a rather British-style spread with not much in the way of concession to yanqui tastes. In his room he read the morning edition of *Ya*, which added meager details regarding Sainz's death to what had been available at *ABC*'s press time the night before. According to one of the servants, the old gentleman had received a telephone call and left his house on foot just after dark. An hour or so later his body had been found in the gutter of Calle Isaac Peral, across from the Institute of Spanish Culture and only two blocks from his house. Tire marks indicated that the death car had jumped the curb and dragged the professor's body some fifteen meters. So far the police had been unable to discover the existence of any witnesses to his death. The driver, when apprehended, would be charged with manslaughter.

The last page of the paper contained formal death notices and tributes, each insertion marked with the customary black formée cross.

Not much for the police to go on, Peter mused as he laid the paper aside, and even less for me. He got up and paced the room while he organized his thoughts. There were certain formalities to be observed, and the sooner he completed them the sooner he could resume his operational plan.

In the florist shop off the lobby Peter ordered two wreaths sent to Sainz's home, one in his name and one in Carberry's, and wrote out cards for each. At the porter's desk he wrote a cable to Professor Carberry, telling him only that Sainz had been killed by an automobile and that he, Peter, was representing them both at the funeral.

It was still too early to call at Sainz's home and sign the funeral book; that would come later in the day, probably not until after he had listened to the apartment's radio receiver for word of some kind from Washington. Hours ago his spoken message had been transcribed in the Langley commo center and copies routed to Hopwood, Sam Perkins, and whoever was sitting in for Avery Thorne.

The jewelry store near the bar entrance was opening its doors, so Peter went in and bought a pair of yellow-gold earrings set with cultured pearls, and asked that they be delivered that evening to Señorita Francisca Borbide at El Guante.

From there he took the elevator to his floor, unlocked his door, and stared in surprise at a man in a short tan raincoat sitting in a chair that faced the door. Peter was about to mumble apologies and withdraw when the man rose and said in Spanish, "No, this is your room. And I advise you to come in."

His rather long hair was silvery gray and neatly combed. Across it lay a thin black ribbon that held a patch in place over his left eye. The hand in his right pocket came out, and it held a flat automatic pistol. He raised his arm, and the barrel pointed at Peter's heart.

Peter blinked. "You must be the man from Hathaway."

"¿Qué?"

"Shirt-sellers," Peter supplied. "Or my former chambermaid's husband?"

The man surveyed him with cold distaste. "I have never married a chambermaid."

"She left in a rush yesterday," Peter said, "having tried unsuccessfully to get me thrown in jail." He drew his glasses from his pocket, put them on, and peered myopically at his visitor.

Very calmly the man said, "I have no idea what you are talking about, and I suggest that you finish closing the door. At once."

Peter estimated his chances of bolting into the hall before the man squeezed the trigger and decided they were nil. Shrugging, he closed the door and leaned back against it.

"Over here." The pistol indicated the direction.

Peter moved slowly across the rug and halted in front of a chair.

"Sit down."

Peter sat down. The man was no fool, no blustering *pistolero*, but one accustomed to giving commands—the right ones—and having them obeyed.

"Now," the man said abruptly, "answer my questions. You saw Profesor Sainz yesterday."

"Yes."

"When did you leave his house?"

"Three-thirty—four."

"Which?"

"I didn't notice. It didn't seem important."

"By seven o'clock last night Professor Sainz was dead—murdered. Where were you at seven o'clock?"

"You're not from the police—why should I tell you?"

The man leaned forward. "You would be well advised to establish your whereabouts convincingly. I have little use for the *policía*, their pedestrian methods, and so I proceed toward truth in my own fashion. Once more: where were you at seven o'clock last night?"

"The Balmoral—the bar on Hermosilla."

"I know it," he said indifferently. "And I know the bartenders well enough to verify your . . . alibi."

Removing his glasses, Peter returned them to his pocket. "I was drinking Canadian Club," he said in a surly voice. "The bartenders ought to remember the only Americano at the bar drinking Canadian Club. Oh yes, I didn't have a poodle. That ought to single me out." He looked hopefully at his interrogator.

"Who introduced you to Don Eduardo—Profesor Sainz?"

"A mutual friend."

"Who?"

Peter drew a carbon copy of his cable from his outside pocket and held it toward the one-eyed man. "Read English?"

"No."

"Well," Peter said, "you wouldn't believe my translation. Maybe we ought to call the hotel interpreter?"

"Idiot!" the man snorted, but he snatched the cable form from Peter's hand. "I will find someone to translate."

"Meanwhile," Peter said, sitting forward, "what are the alternatives? You think I may have caused Sainz's death, while for all I know, you drove the car yourself. You can't check with the Balmoral's bartenders for at least two hours, and you can't put a translator on my cable without leaving here." He stood up slowly. "Are you going to wait here for the next two hours, or are you going to take a chance and shoot me now?"

"You are very clever," the man said sarcastically, "to try to provoke me with your talk of my having killed Don Eduardo—but I recognize it as a ruse to confuse me." He cleared his throat. "You do not confuse me, Señor Ward, because I am older than you, more intelligent than you, and highly experienced in this sort of thing." His thin lips parted in something resembling a smile.

Peter looked at him admiringly. "How did you get in here?"

"A passkey. During our Crusade it was useful to have master keys in one's pocket."

Peter gave a low whistle. "You were a friend of the professor's?"

"A very close friend." The man rose on the balls of his feet and rocked back and forth. He seemed well satisfied with his performance.

"You called the Civil War a crusade," Peter observed, "so you weren't on the Republican side. Were you a Nationalist?"

"At that time," the man grated, "there was hardly a choice."

"And afterward. . . ?"

The man shrugged. "I was—let us say, a friend to Professor Sainz."

Peter nodded. "Don Eduardo told me many interesting things about the Royalist Movement. Perhaps you'd care to tell me more. Take off your coat and stay awhile. I'll order drinks." He started toward the telephone, but a motion of the pistol checked him. Halting, Peter faced the man and swallowed.

He was tiring of his simpleton role, irritated at this one-eyed imitation of a low-echelon *Abwehr* official. Swallowing again, he said, "Well, do we just stand here?"

"You may sit if you like."

The man's visible eye was watering, and Peter waited until one gloved hand raised to blot the moisture away. The blind eye nearly halved the man's peripheral vision, and with the glove interfering—

Dropping to a crouch, Peter snatched up a chair cushion, and as he spun away from the man, let it fly.

The heavy cushion hurtled into the pistol, deflecting it, then into the man's face. He staggered backward, and before he could balance himself Peter kicked his kneecap and slashed the edge of one hand against the gun-holding wrist, numbing it so that the gun dropped to the carpet. As the man dropped to his knees, Peter toed the gun away and kicked the man's left cheek. He groaned, swayed sideways, and would have fallen but for Peter's clutching hands.

Breathing heavily, Peter forced the man back until his head rested on the floor. He leaned his forearm against the man's throat and saw his eye bulge wildly. The man's legs thrashed as he tried to lever himself around and get parallel to Peter, but he was thinking of too many things at once: the pistol on the floor, the forearm crushing his throat, the pain in his wrist, his cheek. . . .

He was strong, Peter realized, but his reflexes had slowed. The contest was between a younger man in good condition and an older, slower man, one used to a gun in the hand.

The body under Peter went limp, the right eye rolled upward like a white carnelian. Peter lifted his forearm and got up. He stood still while his vision cleared, looking for rope, a strap—anything to bind the unconscious man with. After a few moments he opened the closet door and wrenched wire coathangers from the pipe. Untwisting one, he coiled it around the man's ankles, turned him over, and circled his wrists with wire. As he picked up the pistol he heard the man groan breathily. The good eye focused on Peter.

Kneeling beside him, Peter said, "I don't have unlimited patience, *amigo*. Because you're older, more intelligent, and so highly experienced in this sort of thing I'm nervous. I'd remember those things as I pulled the trigger."

He got up, his eyes never leaving the prone man's face.

"You wouldn't . . . kill me," the man blurted.

"*You* came here with a gun—you, not me. *You* told me what was advisable and what was inadvisable. I'd shoot you as a thief and the police would shake my hand." He wet dry lips and sighted down the barrel at the man's belly.

Slowly the man sat up, wrists behind his back. His face contorted, he coughed, and his eye turned up at Peter. "Pull the trigger!"

Peter said nothing.

A thin smile curved the man's lips. "Shoot, eh? I'm not afraid."

Frowning, Peter thumbed the safety and slid the receiver back. No shell ejected. He drew out the magazine, flipped it toward the ceiling, then caught it again. Empty.

Tossing the pistol on the uncushioned chair, he said, "This is the twentieth century. Criminals don't carry empty guns."

"And romantics?"

"Largely killed off." Peter unbuttoned the man's raincoat and reached into his jacket pocket. From it he drew out a gold-embossed green calfskin wallet.

It contained perhaps a thousand pesetas, a small silver rosary, and a Tarjeta de Identidad whose photograph reproduced the face of the man on the floor.

The name given on the card was that of Francisco Herminio Arastegui Ayala, male, born 1913 at Balaguer, province of Gerona. Military service completed.

"Colonel Paco," Peter muttered.

"*¡Señor!*" He inclined his head sardonically.

Turning, Peter walked slowly to the window.

"So," Arastegui called after him, "you know me."

"By name."

"By reputation?"

"By name," Peter repeated. He turned and leaned against the window sill, looking at his prisoner, whose face wore a triumphant smile.

"I am also known as El Tuerto," Arastegui said. "One-eyed. And now that you understand the situation, what are you going to do?"

"The situation? You came here like a vigilante, summarily accusing me of murdering Professor Sainz." He pulled the lobe of one ear. "You knew my name and my address, Paco. Very likely they came from Marisa—"

"The Condesa de Prados," Arastegui interrupted.

Peter shrugged. "She inherited the title on presumption of her father's death. The count has returned, so what her title might be, if any, I wouldn't be able to guess."

"For the present she is the *condesa*."

"All right," Peter said. "If you learned that much you must have learned my business with Sainz. There was no reason to keep it a secret."

"Some legal research sort of thing," he said disdainfully. "Perhaps *sí*, perhaps no. But of one thing I am sure, *señor*, you are not entirely the passive scholar you are supposed to be."

Peter grunted. "What makes you think that?"

Arastegui's bound arms lifted behind him. His chin indicated the wire around his ankles. "You move too fast, too purposefully—almost as though it were second nature."

"You came here with an empty pistol."

"I had an erroneous impression of you."

Leaving the window, Peter picked up the seat cushion, replaced it, and sat in the chair. "I knew Sainz for only a few hours," he said quietly, "but I found him a kind and honorable human being. He was Marisa's foster father and he thought well of you. If you want to forget this incident, I'm willing."

"Agreed."

Kneeling, Peter freed his wrists. Arastegui leaned forward and undid the wire around his ankles. Adjusting his eye patch, he got up slowly and painfully. On his left cheek was an ugly blue swelling.

With a grimace he bent over and began to reassemble the contents of his wallet, then picked up his pistol. Shoving it in his raincoat pocket, he said, "The *profesor* is dead. Will you be staying on in Spain?"

"His archives are available, and there is the National Library." Peter got out his pipe, filled the bowl with tobacco, and lighted it. "When is the funeral?"

"Tomorrow. High Mass at the Iglesia de San Antón. You will attend?"

"I plan to." He drew the pipestem from his mouth. "Will the count be there?"

"I assume so—but no one knows."

"Ill health?"

Arastegui shrugged. "I have not yet seen him, so I cannot testify."

"You knew him twenty years ago?"

"From a distance only."

"And what of his old friends?"

Arastegui cleared his throat. "His close friends are dead, killed in the Cruzada, on the Russian front, or dead from other causes."

Peter bit down on his pipestem. "But you have seen photographs of the count?"

"Only as a very young man. The *milicianos* destroyed nearly all the family relics, you see."

"Professor Sainz knew him well—"

"Very well."

"And would have remembered his appearance, his voice and manner."

"Presumably." Arastegui hesitated. "Are you suggesting something, *señor*?"

Peter shook his head. His visitor began walking toward the door, opened it, and looked back. "Our *profesor*'s remains will be at his home today after three if you care to sign the book."

The door closed behind Arastegui.

After a while Peter threw the door bolt and went to the window. Below, traffic moved up and down San Jerónimo; the sidewalks were filling with tourists, clerks, and office girls. For a time he pondered the circumstances of Sainz's death and Arastegui's strange visit. Then he took the car rental papers from his pocket, studied the signed receipt for his deposit, and called the agency.

"I want to speak to Pablo Martínez Berens."

"¿Pablo?" A quick gasp followed. "Who are you, *señor?*"

"Peter Ward. Yesterday I rented a Mercedes from him, and I—"

"Señor," the voice interrupted, "perhaps I can assist in the matter."

"Where's Pablo?"

"Pablo, Señor Ward, is . . . he is no longer with us."

"He resigned?"

"No, *señor.* Yesterday, completely without authorization, he drove away in one of our cars. This morning at an early hour his body was discovered in the wreckage of the missing vehicle below a cliff seven kilometers this side of San Rafael."

SEVEN

At ten o'clock Langley time (1500 Z), Peter turned on the radio receiver in his apartment, and while the tubes warmed, set the vernier on the day's scheduled wavelength. He tuned the set gradually until he could hear the strains of *Auld Lang Syne* fighting across the Atlantic; then he plugged his tape recorder into the outlet jack and waited for the blind transmission.

It came in the jocular voice of an ostensible ham operator who said, "Old acquaintance should *never* be forgot, and I'm thinking of you, Sarah, when I say that."

Peter smiled.

"I hope you're on my wavelength, Sarah, because Dad asked me to remind you of your promise to visit your cousins. They have a nice place on the beach, you know, and we're sure you'll enjoy it."

Peter looked down at the slowly turning recorder.

"One other thing, Sarah," the voice continued. "We got your cable and Dad says not to worry. He's sending the money, all twenty-three pounds. Get that? Twenty-three pounds. How liberal can a dad be? Well, sister Sarah, that's about all for little ol' now, but you let us hear, hear? *Au-'voir, adiós,* good-bye." Almost at once the melody of *Lisboa Antigua* filtered through the loudspeaker, and Peter listened to a few bars before stopping the recorder and turning off the set.

His message of last night had been received and understood. New instructions or information were being sent him, but he would have to receive them via the Lisbon station (Ralph) at Estoril on the twenty-third.

Today was the twenty-second of the month.

Erasing the backup recording, Peter returned the recorder to the wall safe, which he locked with a spin of the dial.

He had wanted to attend the funeral tomorrow, to see who was there, and to glimpse the count and his daughter. But tomorrow he would be in Portugal.

From Madrid to Lisbon was a jet flight of only an hour, but airline travel lists formed a permanent record available to all too many parties. The Sud-Express left Paris at night, stopped at Madrid in the morning, and reached Lisbon late in the afternoon. It was one of the best trains in Europe, but its schedule was wrong for him and he would have to take a night train to Lisbon.

Peter left the apartment and taxied to the Renfe office on Alcalá, where he reserved a compartment on the Lisbon sleeper that left Atocha station at midnight. Tickets in his pocket, he took another taxi to Calle Eslava and got out in front of the brownstone house whose doorway was now draped and outlined with sashes of black crepe.

Inside, visitors were filing slowly past the closed, flower-banked casket in the sitting room. Behind the casket hung the flags, banners, and guidons of the cause to which the old scholar had dedicated his life.

Peter joined the line and moved around the coffin, pausing to read the inscription engraved on a silver plate affixed to the glassed-in plaque that contained the blue *boina* he had noticed the day before. The legend read: *Beret worn by the Excelentísimo Sr. Conde de Prados at the battle of Belchite, August 25, 1937, against the XVth International Brigade.*

Passing on, he went through a doorway that led into another room, where visitors were signing the register on a table set with lighted candles, a large silver crucifix, and a statue of the Virgin.

When he had signed his name, Peter moved toward the

rear of the house and saw Paco Arastegui in conversation with a tall, gaunt, mustachioed old man from whose shoulders hung a black cape.

El Tuerto was dressed in black suit, tie, and shoes, and the bruise on his cheek had turned dark purple. Moving casually in his direction, Peter saw Arastegui's eye settle on him. The Royalists' paramilitary chief broke off his conversation and limped toward Peter. He said emotionally, "Did you hear the news?"

"What news?"

"The man who killed Don Eduardo?"

Peter shook his head, and Arastegui drew him aside to let a group of students pass.

"His name was Martínez," Arastegui whispered. "Only God knows why he killed Don Eduardo, for he is dead himself. Disgracefully, he was a member of our Movement, a *cabo* in our Brigade."

"How do they know it was Martínez?"

"The evidence on his car—the blood and hair of Don Eduardo adhering to its metal." He shook his head bleakly.

"Perhaps his hitting Professor Sainz was an accident and he killed himself in remorse," Peter suggested.

"That is, of course, possible—but given the world in which we live I cannot discard the possibility of conspiracy."

Peter would have widened the opening had not the tall man with whom Arastegui had been conversing approached them.

"I must leave, Paco," he said solemnly as they clasped hands.

Arastegui nodded, then said, "Don Felipe, this is the American of whom I spoke. Dr. Ward, Don Felipe Carbajal."

"Mucho gusto." Peter extended his hand.

"The pleasure is mine," said Carbajal in ponderous Spanish, "and it would be greater were it not for the sorrowful occasion of our meeting."

In a low voice Arastegui said, "Don Felipe is the *impulsor* of our Movement."

"Yes," Peter said, "so Don Eduardo told me."

"A noble man," Carbajal intoned, and touched one liver-speckled cheek. Turning to Arastegui, he said, "I leave Marisa in your hands, Paco." Then he bowed to Peter and moved slowly toward the front of the house.

Peter said, "The *condesa* is here?"

"In the library. But she is overcome with grief—I would not—"

"I can do no less than extend my sympathy," Peter told him. *"Con permiso."*

"Pase," the Spaniard said curtly, and Peter walked on down the hall.

The library door was partly open. Through it Peter could see a section of stacked bookshelves; he heard the low murmur of a woman's voice. Knocking, he entered and saw Marisa sitting in a chair beside Sainz's desk. She was dressed entirely in black and her face was veiled. Behind the desk, his head barely visible above the piles of paper, sat a man gazing into the garden below.

Without moving, Marisa said, "Dr. Ward?"

"Forgive me for intruding, *condesa,* but I wanted to pay my respects to you and express my deepest sympathy."

"Thank you."

"Don Eduardo told me how much you meant to him, and I—"

"Yes. I looked on him as a father, loved him as a father." One hand touched the hem of her veil, behind which her eyes barely showed.

Her head moved slightly in the direction of the seated man. Raising her voice, she said, "Father."

The man behind the desk turned his head, showing a strong profile with a prominent, curved nose and deep-set eyes. Angling across his cheekbone was a concave scar.

"Father," she repeated in Spanish, "may I present Dr. Ward?"

"Dr. . . . Ward," he murmured in remote, accented syllables.

Peter took a step toward him, then halted when the count did not move. In English he said, "He must be deeply affected, *condesa*. Perhaps some other time."

"You are most considerate," she said in English. "As you may have heard, the horrors he survived left their imprint on his mind—though perhaps not permanently."

"Let us hope not." Peter noticed that the count was facing the garden window once more. "So green," the count murmured. "Everything so green . . ."

Marisa's head turned as though to deflect the childish words.

Peter said, *"Condesa,* might I have your permission to continue my work here among your archives?"

"If you desire."

"I would have delayed my request until after the services tomorrow, but unfortunately I must spend a few days in Portugal."

"If I can be of help to you after your return, we will be at our *finca.*"

"Muy agradecido."

"I appreciate your courtesy in coming, Doctor."

"Don Eduardo showed me unusual kindness, *condesa.* Again, my most profound sympathy." Bowing, he left the room.

On his way down the corridor, Peter glanced into the room that held the casket of Eduardo Sainz, and saw a young woman kneeling beside it, her veil drawn. Her pale face had a brooding madonnalike quality that attracted his interest, and he paused while her lips moved in silent prayer. Their eyes met. Peter nodded uncomfortably and went out to the street.

The Spanish police had moved rapidly in linking the battered car of Pablo Martínez to the death of Professor Sainz, but as Arastegui had indicated, Pablo's motive was still unknown. Peter walked toward the university, wondering if his telephoning Sainz within earshot of Martínez had triggered the old man's murder in some oblique way. The odds were heavily against it, particularly since Martínez had been a member of the Royalist Movement, and a corporal in Arastegui's militia. Still, doubt would trouble him until the truth was known—if it were ever known.

Reaching Calle de Isaac Peral, Peter turned right and walked north in front of the Instituto de Cultura Hispánica until he saw on the sidewalk an X marked in yellow chalk. Dark stains surrounded it. the lifeblood of Eduardo Sainz, and the nearby cobbles were streaked with the black marks of skidding tires. The visual evidence pointed to hit-and-run, but it was no accident; rather, a calculated slaying so cleverly designed that even the killer was dead. Liquidated.

Liquidated, Peter mused; Soviet terminology, and his mind re-created the head and shoulders of the Conde de Prados, the strong profile, withdrawn eyes, and scarred cheek. He remembered the count's few words with their dull, childish inflection, and thought that either the count was a powerfully competent actor, or his mind had been sapped, damaged—perhaps beyond healing and repair. The few photographs of the count that Peter had seen had been taken when he was comparatively young—during the Civil War and World War II. Strong similarities existed between the photographs and the man Peter had glimpsed with Marisa in the library. And as for the facial scar, it was long established that the count had been wounded at Vitebsk by shrapnel in a manner to account for the scar.

Could it be, Peter wondered, that Thorne's suspicions were groundless, that his mission in Madrid was a useless, sleeveless errand? An easy and logical explanation was that all reports of the count's death in a *siblag* were hearsay, that he had been shifted from one camp to another in such a way as to prevent barracks comrades from learning of his existence. And then, in convoluted Soviet fashion, a credible story of his death had been circulated.

It was possible that the Soviets had held the count in secrecy against the day when a live Conde de Prados might be useful as a pawn in some obscure, tangential KGB maneuver. It was equally possible that during twenty years' imprisonment the count had been converted to the Soviet cause; that he had become, in fact, a Soviet agent.

But what returns could the Soviets expect from an agent whose actions so strongly suggested severe mental impairment? Peter's impression of the count was of a man in a tomb, a cataleptic, a mute, volitionless, being indifferent to his surroundings. The Russian word for such a person was *dokhodyaga*—a goner, a burned-out wick. And that was far from describing even the average Soviet agent.

Peter was close to being persuaded that the man who had returned from Vorkuta was the Conde de Prados, aged forty years in the twenty chronological years of his absence. A standard Soviet procedure was to release far-gone or aged prisoners to the care of their family, for the physically and mentally incapable represented a deficit to the *siblag* bookkeeping system; they ate but they did not work.

Only two factors prevented Peter from rendering a positive judgment on the count to Headquarters: the curious absence of persons who had known the count well in his youth; and the murder of Professor Sainz, occurring as it had in time to eliminate a scheduled meeting between the two old friends.

Shaking his head, Peter thought: We can't close the case file yet. Not quite yet.

Then he became aware of footsteps behind him: precise steps whose pace was more rapid than his own. He slowed his walk and listened for a moment, thinking the other steps might slow also, but they kept on, and from their timbre he realized that—

"Dr. Ward!"

Halting, he turned. A woman. The young woman he had seen kneeling at the foot of the professor's coffin.

"Dr. Ward," she repeated as she reached him. She stopped and took a deep breath. "I am—allow me to introduce myself—Beatriz Peralta."

Peter took one black-gloved hand. *"Encantado,"* he said, and saw a troubled expression on her face.

"You—you do not know me? My name?"

"I'm afraid not."

"Yesterday when you telephoned Profesor—Sainz," she

said haltingly, "I spoke with you, arranged your luncheon with the *profesor*. Now do you remember?"

"Of course."

"You were calling from the car rental agency."

"So I was."

She moved to his right, and Peter fell in step beside her. "I had hoped to meet you yesterday, Doctor, then . . ." One gloved hand lifted to her eyes. "It was kind of you to come to the house today, genuinely kind, even though you had known my father only a short time."

"Your *father*? You said your name is Peralta."

She nodded slowly, hesitantly. "In Spain . . . it is the custom when one's . . . one's parents are not married to use the . . . mother's name."

Peter felt himself color. "I apologize."

"Please . . . so even though I am . . . *ilegítima* I am the daughter of . . . the late Profesor Sainz." Turning, she glanced back at the sidewalk's yellow cross, and began to sob. Peter tried to comfort her while the spasm ran its course. Then, drying her eyes, Beatriz Peralta spoke in a frayed, uneven voice. "Not many people know why Pablo killed my father as he did."

"And you do?"

"I—*I* am the cause of it, *señor*. Pablo loved me—or said he did—but my father objected to our marrying. You see, Pablo had no university degree—not even a *bachillerato*—and my father, Don Eduardo, thought him uneducated and unacceptable. He—my father—was fifty-five when I was born, you see. My mother was his housekeeper—herself an uneducated servant woman from Navarre. So—" Her voice tightened and she turned away, shoulders trembling. "Dr. Ward," she said huskily, "please feel free to work in the archives after—after the services tomorrow. That is what I wanted to tell you, but also I had to leave the house—I, I had to leave that place where I had no legal right to be—no more right than any of those who came today as mourners."

"I understand," Peter said quietly. "You loved Pablo Martíncz?"

"Whatever I may have felt for him," she said in a controlled voice, "I hate him now. If there is a hell, I want him to burn in it everlastingly. Ah . . . *Dios* . . ."

Grief overcame her, and as they entered the broad plaza of Cristo Rey, he put an arm around her shoulders to steady her steps. The tables of a sidewalk café were only a few meters away, so he guided her to one, and as the waiter came up he ordered brandy for both of them. Nodding understandingly, the waiter hurried away, returning shortly with a tray bearing two glasses and a sealed bottle of Lepanto, which he opened. Peter filled their glasses. Beatriz lifted hers, smiled wanly, and said, "Thank you, Doctor."

"Pedro," he suggested.

"Pedro." She sipped from the glass and gazed at him. Her eyes were unusually large, he saw, even with the puffiness around them that came from tears. Or perhaps it was an illusion fostered by the contrast of her pale skin and concave cheeks. Almost an El Greco face in its elongation, he mused, sipped from his glass, and felt rewarded by the smoothness of the liqueur.

After a while Beatriz murmured, "I feel much better now —thanks to you."

Peter added brandy to her glass.

"Don Pedro—" she began hesitatingly, "I—would you escort me to the funeral tomorrow?"

"I wish I could, *mi hija*, but I must leave Madrid for some days."

"I see—and I understand. It was . . . forward of me to make the request, but I—" Her eyes lowered. "May I ask where it is you go? To the countryside, perhaps?"

"Yes—a distance from Madrid." Having taken steps to insure an unobserved departure for Portugal, Peter saw no compelling reason to confide his destination to anyone—even the daughter of the late Professor Sainz. "One of the provincial libraries," he added as an afterthought.

"Alcalá de Henares?"

"León. The archivist has been good enough to grant me a period of consultation; unfortunately it cannot be postponed."

"Then you must go," she said quietly, "and I will see you when you return. Having helped my father so long, I may be able to assist your work as well."

"Very possibly." Taking out his watch, he glanced at it, then said, "May I see you to your . . . apartment?"

"I do not wish to detain you longer, Pedro. Perhaps a taxi . . . ?"

Peter signaled the waiter, paid the small bill, and asked him to flag a taxi. As he helped Beatriz inside she laid a gloved hand on his. "Again, thank you, Pedro. I"—she faltered, then resumed—"being with you has helped—a great deal."

He closed the door, stepped back onto the sidewalk, and watched the taxi drive away.

Walking up Calle de San Francisco de Sales he pondered the encounter with Beatriz Peralta, her self-identification as the bastard daughter of Eduardo Sainz, and her explanation of the motive for his death. Peter justified his indirection with her for two disturbing reasons. First, if it had been she who first spoke with him from the Sainz home, he did not recall having named the agency as the place from which he was calling—though Pablo Martínez could have informed her after the fact that day; and second, Sainz had described himself as childless.

Ahead a taxi stood by the curb, the driver dozing in the shadows of the waning afternoon. Peter woke him, got inside, and settled back on the rear seat. As the taxi headed east toward Espalter Peter reflected that if Sainz had fathered an illegitimate daughter, his ingrained sense of honor would have prevented him from describing himself as childless. Sainz would never have mentioned the subject at all.

The ripples widen, Peter mused, and decided that he ought to look into the background and associations of Miss Beatriz Peralta as soon as he got back from Lisbon.

EIGHT

Lisbon in the brilliant morning sunlight was a wanton child garbed in soft pastels of blue, green, and yellow; provocatively tawny flesh and vermilion mouth sweet with spice and the fragrance of fresh *café*. The planes of her seven hills seemed to alter with the rhythmically undulating motion of Peter's horse-drawn fiacre, and now she was a dusty, ravaged harlot, rank-smelling and tattered; as suddenly she was verdant again and young. A bewildering city, Peter told himself, involved in endless change, with only the Tagus, the Castelo, and the Rocio constant to their abiding past.

The night train had taken him through Torrijos and Navalmoral to Garrovillas and the frontier; now the *clop-clop* of horses' hooves was a soothing change from the *nickety-rack, nickety-rack* of the rails. Breakfast in the dining compartment had been early and incomplete: fruit, brioche, and coffee, and the fiacre was now taking him to the Ritz Hotel for a postscript that would hold to his sinews through the day ahead.

The hotel entrance faced Eduardo VII Park. When he had walked into the lobby he asked the porter to check his bag, then entered the dining room, where a few sedate and elderly guests were seated in green plush armchairs.

After tropical melon and kippers Peter launched into wild-hog bacon with its unmistakable nutty savor, eggs, hot breads, and syrupy Portuguese coffee. As he rose, replete, he felt that whatever the day might hold, dining need not be one of his worries.

By then it was ten o'clock, and because the embassy was closed on Saturdays, he dialed an alternate contact number from a booth telephone, asked the answering servant for the master of the house, and heard, after a short wait, the voice of Johnston Petty.

"*Olá*—Petty speaking."

"*Olá* yourself. How are things in Glocamorra?"

"In Gloc—?" The recognition phrase seemed to have lodged in the distant reaches of Petty's mind. "Oh," he said finally. "Very well. Staying long?"

"It depends."

"Then I suggest the beaches. You'll like the Estoril Palácio—veddy international, if you like that kind of thing."

"I don't fight it."

"Well, I went ahead and got you a room there. Go on out and have a swim—I'll stop by for lunch about one."

"I'm glad things proceed here at a leisurely pace," Peter said a little irritably. "Where I've come from it's like Fourth of July at the fairgrounds."

"I'm a city boy myself," Petty said blandly. "*Boa viagem*—see you later." Considerably later, Peter groused, as he left the booth. He found the porter, asked him to load his bag into a taxi, changed pesetas for escudos, and was shortly heading over the Auto-Estrada past the stadium in the direction of Estoril. The old houses had conical turrets, colored tiles, and wrought-iron balconies, and the roof ends were turned up pagoda-style—to avert the Evil Eye, according to tradition. On his left flowed the Tagus estuary, its color greening gradually, while the old fortress of Caxias peered over the road as they neared the town of Oeiras. Peter could see umbrella pines and *spinde* trees; along the roadside camellias, ferns, and periwinkle grew wild, and the air smelled of resin and peat, with a faint sea-born scent of iodine.

The vineyards of Carcavelos descended to the road, and beyond he could see small fishing settlements strung with ochre nets. Women in shawls and men in stocking caps clustered around the gaudily painted high-prowed boats, each decorated, like Chinese junks, with a watchful eye.

Lighting his pipe, Peter smoked and drowsed for a few minutes; then he alerted himself as the road dropped down into Estoril, its long reach of fine sand dotted with colorful umbrellas and beach chairs. Palm trees played host to climbing roses, and beyond them stood the Estoril Palácio, serene under the midday sun.

His room was on the ocean side with a good view of

the beach and rolling surf, and when he had unpacked he ordered drinks for himself and Petty, slowly sipped a Canadian Club, and began writing a long cable to Headquarters.

When he had finished he looked down at the beach again and considered a swim, but he preferred warm waters; at this time of year Estoril's beach was enjoyed principally by Germans and Scandinavians. There was wind as well, and a tricky undertow even on comparatively calm days, so Peter passed up the opportunity. As he lay back on the bed, he remembered that it was Saturday and that he had a *compromiso* with Paquí in Madrid.

Paquí, he thought, and smiled. When he did not appear at El Guante she would go off with the most presentable male who asked her, and wear his earrings in the bargain. It had been two years since his first meeting with Paquí in Barcelona, and he did not want another two years to slip by without the pleasure of her company.

A little after twelve, Johnston Petty called Peter's room from the lobby, came up and knocked on the door. Peter let him in, they shook hands, and Peter said, "You're early."

Petty shrugged. He was younger than Peter and junior in rank; he had a slight build and a rather rustic face. Pulling a sealed envelope from his pocket, he handed it to Peter. "This third-country contacting is fine for you traveling salesmen, but for us locals it's not too restful."

"I've been a local myself," Peter said soothingly. "Mix yourself a drink."

"I will at that, and I'll have time to drink it, too. There's a lot of stuff for you to read. My commo guy was up half the night decoding that last Priority."

"Me blackfella b'long numbah one boss man, same-same you. Which translated means we all drink from the same well." Peter opened the envelope, set the three cables in chronological order, and read them at the writing desk.

The first message acknowledged his radio transmission and asked for a status report plus any thoughts he might have regarding the significance of Sainz's murder. The second cable referenced the first and asked that he transmit a psychological assessment of the count as soon as development reached that point. Peter shook his head and heard Petty chuckle. "I laughed at that one myself, Peter."

"Yeah. How do you psychologically assess a man who looks and acts as if he'd been fallen on by a tree?"

"Easy—you ask Headquarters to send over a shrinker to lighten your task. It's spring, comrade, when travel fever hits even Medical Division."

Peter nodded, pushed the cable aside, and saw that the next one was stamped *Priority* in purple ink, and was slugged

Sensitive. It began: INFO PASS SERAPH, and its text was:

A. TEHERAN STATION REPORTS COL. SERGEI NIKOLAI VOLKOV, GRU * SPETS BYURO, NOT SEEN TEHERAN LAST THREE WEEKS. ABSENT FROM MILITARY ATTACHÉ LUNCHEONS AND OTHER AFFAIRS.

B. UNDER BERIA HEADED MVD SECTION WITH AUTHORITY OVER FORCED LABOR SYSTEM. SINCE THEN VOLKOV HAS BECOME WELL KNOWN SPECIAL OPS MAN WITH CONSIDERABLE EXPERIENCE DIRECTING ILLEGAL REZIDENTURAS, PRINCIPALLY IN MIDDLE EAST. VOLKOV SAID TO BE CLOSE TO GEN. IVASHUTIN, HEAD OF GRU, THOUGH KREMLIN POWER SHAKEUP MAY MAKE IVASHUTIN'S POSITION UNCERTAIN.

C. VOLKOV PNG-D CANBERRA 1956, ATHENS 1958. LEFT THE HAGUE AFTER FOREIGN MINISTRY WARNING IN WAKE ATTEMPTED POISONING LEADER HUNGARIAN EXILE GROUP 1961. CONSIDERED RESOURCEFUL AND RUTHLESS.

D. RELIABLE OBSERVER REPORTS VOLKOV TRANSITED ROME AIRPORT IN MUFTI APRIL 3 EN ROUTE PARIS. NO CONFIRMATION THIS OR SUBSEQUENT ARRIVAL PARIS. CHECKING COPENHAGEN, STOCKHOLM, AND OSLO.

E. IN VIEW PRADOS CASE PECULIARITIES PLUS VIOLENT DEATH EDUARDO SAINZ FEEL NOT IMPOSSIBLE VOLKOV INVOLVED. PHYSICAL DESCRIPTION: HT 5′ 9″; WT 174 LBS; EYES DARK; SKIN SOMEWHAT YELLOWISH; HAIR BLACK, USUALLY CUT SHORT. MOUSTACHE ON OCCASION. SCAR ON RIGHT FOREARM. GENERAL APPEARANCE MONGOLIAN AND HEFTY.

Peter looked up from the cable.

Setting aside his drink, Petty said, "I like that touch about the forearm scar. I can see you bracing suspicious characters all over Madrid, rolling up their right sleeves despite vigorous protests."

"It's a shot in the dark," Peter commented. "I suppose every time a Sov drops out of sight we'll hear about it."

"Yeah. Well, that's one thing about Lisboa, comrade, Soviets is one thing we ain't got. Ready for lunch?"

Peter pulled a sheet of paper from the drawer and wrote

* Glavnoye Razedyvatelnoye Upravleniye—Chief Intelligence Directorate (military).

another cable to Headquarters asking for traces on Pablo Martínez Berens, age at death about twenty-seven; and Beatriz Peralta, age about twenty-four; alleged illegitimate daughter of Eduardo Sainz. Handing the incoming and outgoing cables to Petty, he said, "Let's go."

Petty scanned his drafts, folded the batch, and put it in his inside jacket pocket. "You didn't respond to the shrinker cable."

"Possibly tomorrow. I don't want just any junior Jung clanking around Madrid—there's a gourd-shaker I've worked with before, a solid man who speaks Spanish and Russian."

"Sol Podret?"

"The same. Now show me what's so great about Estoril."

Luncheon began with *mexilhões,* small fresh clams; progressed to *ensopado,* a thick meat soup; moved on to *lula,* pilaff of squid; and wound up with *queijo de Azeitão,* goat cheese, and orange cake and coffee. Port went with the first course, then a chilled bottle of *vinho verde* that reminded Peter of Austria's scarce Gumpoldskirchner.

After their meal they strolled along the beach walk for exercise, rested on the wall to talk, and returned to Peter's room.

Petty said, "I've got the commo man standing by, so I'd best get your messages on the air." He glanced at his wristwatch. "It's only ten o'clock at Headquarters; you'll probably get replies tomorrow. If you don't, there are worse places to pass a weekend than Estoril."

"Much worse," Peter agreed, shook hands with Petty, and saw him to the door.

For the rest of the afternoon he slept, waking to see a slim red crescent of the sun on the Atlantic horizon. The wind had dropped and the ocean rolled with long dark swells. To the north the ocean was flecked with the carbide lights of fishing boats setting out from shore.

It was a tranquil and pleasant scene that recalled summer nights at Gloucester when he was a boy walking along Ministers' Row, watching schooners manned by men of Portuguese blood put out to sea.

After a shower and a shave he put on a lightweight dinner jacket and went down to the bar, where a *fado* singer was strolling among the tables with his guitar. Gradually a crowd of well-dressed, attractive-looking people assembled, reminding Peter that Portugal was the final refuge of Europe's displaced royalty, many of whom lived year-round at Estoril. The Spanish pretender lived there, along with several pages of the Almanach de Gotha in better or lesser circumstances.

Peter lingered over two highballs for an hour; then, wearied of the singer's inconclusive lament, he went into the dining room for a dinner of jugged lobster and prawns. After that he drifted into the casino, played *chemin de fer* until he had won something under four thousand escudos, drank a nightcap in the nearby bar, and was in bed before midnight.

The morning sea was calm and the sun so bright that Peter went into the water and swam half an hour before breakfast, which was served on the terrace overlooking the beach. An early riser for Estoril, Peter had beach and the terrace nearly to himself, and after the press of the casino he enjoyed the morning's comparative solitude. Breakfast over, he stretched out on his balcony and soaked up sun until the telephone rang.

"Peter? Johnston Petty here."

"What news?"

"Show you in half an hour. Just wanted to make sure you'd be there."

Peter took another twenty minutes of sun, put on a bathrobe, and ordered coffee sent to the room. Petty arrived on schedule, handed Peter a sealed envelope, and poured a *bica,* which he sipped slowly while Peter read the incoming cables.

There was a *pro forma* admonition against Peter's proceeding too rapidly under what Headquarters construed as altered circumstances. "Roger," he muttered, "noted in passing," laid the cable aside, and read the next. Neither Paris, Copenhagen, Stockholm, nor Oslo could verify the presence of Colonel Volkov, and Peter reflected that most likely Volkov had been recalled to Moscow. With the departure of Nikita, the life expectancy of GRU holdovers from the Beria era was becoming increasingly conjectural, and Peter was inclined to discard Volkov's personal intervention in Spain as a serious possibility.

The third cable reflected no traces on Beatriz Peralta, but concerning Pablo Martínez Berens it said quite a lot.

Pablo had been born in 1939 at Manresa in Cataluña to parents who were militant Anarcho-Syndicalists and active in the defense of Barcelona. After the Republican defeat they had followed the refugee stream to Port Bou on the French frontier, and thence to Marseilles, where the Soviet ship *Kursk* transported them to Odessa. Of the parents nothing further was known, but in 1957 a man purporting to be Pablo Martínez Berens applied for repatriation to Spain as a native-born Spaniard, and was granted an exit permit by the Soviet authorities. There was no record of his having attended a GRU or KGB training school; consequently no follow-up surveillance by the Seguridad Nacional. Martínez had simply dropped from sight, blending among 2 million other *madrileños* until the morning of his death.

A Niño.

Laying aside the cable, Peter reached for his pipe and filled it. Petty got up and stared down at the Martínez cable. "Like it, Peter?"

"I don't know," he said moodily.

"With that kind of background, Martínez must have been under Soviet direction. Then, when he'd killed Sainz, he was liquidated by his superior. Clean; no dusty trails, no sticky hands. That's the Sovs for you. Inexpensive disposal and no chance of flareback."

"And who minds a little gore?"

"Yeah." Petty finished his *bica* and put down the empty cup. "There's a Portuguese Airways Caravelle to Madrid at four o'clock—it hits Barajas about six. Nothing else until morning."

"I'll take it."

"Stout fella. Flight 704—the desk can book you."

"I'd just as soon not broadcast my travel plans."

"Sure—airport's just as good."

Peter returned his cables to the Lisbon Chief of Station and said, "Sorry to put you to all this trouble."

"It's becoming a way of life," Petty said resignedly, shook hands with Peter, and left.

After lunch Peter took a taxi back over the fifteen-mile drive to Lisbon and got out at the Central Railway station, where he telephoned the airline and reserved a seat on the flight to Madrid. Then he carried his bag out to a fiacre, hired the carriage for an hour, and settled back to watch the Sunday afternoon crowds along Avenida da Liberdade, as the fiacre moved gradually toward Eduardo VII Park. After a turn around the park, the driver headed south to the river, passing Rocio Square with its hundreds of strolling couples, then rounded the vast Praça do Commercio, which reminded Peter of the Place de la Concorde.

It was here, at the edge of the Tagus, that refugees from Central Europe waited weeks and months on end for passage to the New World, lying on the stones or huddled on the benches that now held a few young couples and elderly people drowsing in the afternoon sun.

Returning to the station, Peter paid the driver, went inside, and found a taxi at the opposite entrance. From there to Portela Airport was a short trip, and he arrived in plenty of time to buy his ticket and go through exit formalities before Flight 704 was called.

Aloft, he ate a sandwich and drank a highball, dozed for an hour, and was wakened as the Caravelle began its approach descent. The landing was smooth and Barajas uncrowded. He passed rapidly through immigration, police, and customs, exchanged his remaining escudos for Spanish pesetas, and was in the Palace Hotel by seven.

At the desk he asked for his key, and with it was given a cable and a small white envelope bearing an engraved coat of arms. The cable was from Professor Carberry, expressing regret over Sainz's death and thanking Peter for notifying him. The envelope contained a guest card to the Club Real de Puerta de Hierro, signed by María Luisa Pérez y Vals Delgado, Condesa de Prados. It was a generous gesture, Peter thought, for the Puerta de Hierro was Madrid's most fashionable club, and its twenty-seven-hole course was unexcelled in Spain.

A bellboy carried Peter's bag to the lift, rode with him to the fourth floor, and unlocked the door. A box of clean laundry occupied the luggage rack, so Peter said, "Just put it on the bed and I'll take care of it later." He felt in his pocket for a tip.

Lifting the bag, the boy dropped it on the bed.

In that moment the bed seemed to lift. Fangs of flame shot from under it and an ear-splitting detonation hurled Peter against the wall. Dazedly he got to his knees and peered through the choking smoke at flames spurting upward from the broken bed.

From the torn and blackened body of the boy.

NINE

The name of the dead boy was José Perdomo. Born in Maqueda, he had passed his seventeenth birthday only three weeks before, and had been well-regarded by other employees and the management. The information was given to the police by a distraught assistant manager in the hotel's first-aid room while Peter's cuts and bruises were being dressed. His hair and eyebrows had been singed by the blast, and his left shoulder felt as if it had been dislocated from the impact of his body against the wall. One knee hurt, and a stitch had been taken to close a cut over his left eyebrow.

When the manager left the plainclothes detective said, "You were most fortunate, *señor*."

Peter lifted a shot-glass portion of pain-killer and gulped the evil-tasting compound.

"We depend heavily on your assistance, *señor*," the detective went on. "Clearly the dynamite bomb was intended for you. Who would want to kill you?"

"I don't know."

The detective's eyes narrowed. "A young man is dead, Señor Ward, and justice demands the life of his murderer. I ask you again: what enemies do you have who could have contrived this monstrous affair?"

Peter shook his head. Dazed as he was, he had decided to say as little as he could. The police had a murder to solve, but the solution—if one ever emerged—lay with the counter-intelligence section of Seguridad Nacional. And to preserve the security of his own operation, he could give them no leads, no help at all.

"Surely," the detective was saying, "it is only logical to assume from the facts that the bomb was intended for your destruction. It was your bed, *señor*, your room."

Peter licked dry, puffed lips. "The miners of Asturias know the uses of dynamite."

"*Sí*. But do you know any Asturian miners who wish your death?"

Peter shrugged, and the movement pained his injured shoulder; it was a gesture he would have to use sparingly. "Spain is not free of terrorist incidents. The death of an American tourist would make good anti-Spanish propaganda abroad."

The detective cleared his throat. "You suggest that you were merely a random objective?"

"I have no other explanation."

"And you"—he glanced down delicately at his hands—"are no more than an ordinary American tourist?"

"I don't understand the question."

He picked up Peter's passport and leafed through the pages. "Given the number of countries you have visited within the past three years, it appears that you are singularly devoted to tourism."

Time for a new passport, Peter said to himself; the documentation lads were getting careless. "I was representing a group of investors interested in establishing a chain of international hotels."

"And that is why you were in Barcelona two years ago?"

Peter swallowed. He had been in Barcelona on the Pallicini affair, but he said, "That had to do with certain shipbuildng contracts."

The detective closed the passport but gave no indication of returning it. "I find it very hard to believe," he said at length, "that you are as innocent of all knowledge as you appear. I wonder if a stay in our prison might not improve your memory."

"On what charge?"

"As a material witness—or as a suspect."

Peter sucked in a deep breath. "Do what you must," he said dully.

The detective sat forward, his eyes narrowing. "Do you want to communicate with the American consul?"

"I have no reason to. As to legal questions I am a lawyer, and the consul, very likely, is not." His head throbbed; he felt shaky and nauseated as the memory of the boy's burning body flooded his mind.

In Cairo six years before, his wife had been killed in their bedroom by a plastic charge meant for him, and the lingering stench of gelignite in his nostrils brought the scene starkly back.

His jaw set, he closed his eyes and tried to massage away the vision. Then the door opened and footsteps approached.

Opening his eyes, he saw another plainclothesman whisper to the detective and hand him a large filing card. The detective scanned the card and turned to Peter.

"Señor Ward, do you have any reason to suspect that the one responsible for the attempt on your life is Señora Mercedes del Carmen Abreu?"

"Who is she?"

"The chambermaid who allegedly left a Communist leaflet in your room." He gestured at the filing card. "Seguridad Nacional recorded the episode on her *ficha*."

"Do women usually handle dynamite?"

"It happens."

Peter wet his lips. "Ask her."

"We intend to, *señor*—when we find her. It seems she has not been seen at the hotel since the day you were interviewed by Teniente Quiroga of the Seguridad Nacional."

"It might be a lead," Peter said noncommittally.

"Enough that I am disinclined to hold you, *señor*." He returned the *ficha* to his subordinate and got up. "The lady comes from Asturias," he said in a thoughtful voice. "Perhaps you would be willing to assist in our investigation?"

"In what way?"

"By remaining out of sight for a time. Long enough—let us say—to regain your normal appearance."

Peter touched the bandage over his eye, the cut on his cheek. "How will that help?"

In patient tones the detective said, "No notice of the bombing will appear in the press; hotel employees will be warned not to speak of it, and your room restored to its normal condition. If the *dinamitero* thinks the bomb has not exploded he may be tempted to return to your room and examine the charge." He smiled thinly. "If he does, he will be seized."

Peter shook his head. "I don't think your plan will work. People in nearby rooms heard the explosion, saw the body being taken away. They'll talk about it. One of the guests may even have been the bomber."

"I do not know about your country, *señor*, but in Spain *dinamiteros* do not lodge at the Palace Hotel."

There was no point in arguing, Peter reflected. The Civil War stereotype of a dynamiter as a red-shirted *campesino* with a bandoleer over one shoulder was fixed and immutable. Even so, if the affair could be suppressed, the lack of publicity would serve him vis-à-vis the Royalists. If Marisa or El Tuerto—even Beatriz Peralta—learned of the attempt on his life they would regard him with curiosity and suspicion. To win their confidence he had to appear to be no more and no less than his cover legend prescribed.

As yet none of his contacts knew of his return to Madrid. He could simply withdraw until his appearance was normal once more, then resume his former ways. For those reasons, rather than the detective's, he said, "I'll cooperate."

"*¡Bueno!*" The detective rose, took a card from his pocket, and handed it to Peter. Printed on it was his name: Fermín Hernández, and a telephone number. "Let me know when you return to Madrid, Señor Ward." He took out a cigarette, lighted it, and blew smoke at the white ceiling. "Where do you think you will go? The Costa del Sol? Majorca?"

"I would be too conspicuous in these bandages. Is the Parador at Gredos open?"

"Assuredly it is—and the fishing is reported to be superb. I will be glad to reserve accommodations for you."

"Thanks, but I'll take care of it." Peter wanted no police taint to precede him at Gredos.

They shook hands and the detective left the room.

The doctor finished washing his hands, dried them, and walked over to Peter. "Live quietly for a time, *señor*," he advised. "Avoid violent exercise, and in three days the stitch may be withdrawn." Removing his spectacles, he folded them in the breast pocket of his coat. "You were exceptionally fortunate to escape with your life. Had the boy not—" He broke off and shrugged. "These things are in the hands of *nuestro Señor*, is it not so?"

Peter nodded. The potion was taking effect and the pain was duller now, a pulsing throb in his head and back. He took five $100 traveler's checks from his wallet, countersigned them, and handed them to the physician.

"Tonight José Perdomo was my surrogate, Doctor. This

should cover his burial with perhaps something for his family."

"Yes—indeed, it will, *señor*, and you are most generous. The hotel and the state will make the statutory payment to his survivors, but this . . . this gift of yours exceeds—"

Peter lifted one hand and got to his feet. "I trust to your discretion," he said, and went out to the corridor.

By walking slowly he was able to minimize the pain, though his steps were unsteady and the wall a useful guide. From above came the strains of dance music, the clatter of dishes in the hotel kitchen. He made his way to the rear basement exit and climbed a ramp to the street.

Cool air stung his face. Shivering, he walked as far as the Paseo and took a taxi to Calle Espalter. Riding the lift to his apartment, he debated letting Headquarters know about the incident, fearing he would be recalled and replaced with a less vulnerable substitute. But even if Hernández was able to prevent publicity over the bombing, the station undoubtedly had its own sources within the hotel, if not within the Madrid police. And so he decided to notify Langley, giving his own interpretation of what had happened, and describing his cooperation with the police.

The transmitter was safe in the vault, but Peter preferred a less immediate means of communication. His shaving kit with its secret-writing compound had been destroyed in the blast, along with everything else in the bag. But from his remaining bag he got out a tube of cotton-tipped throat swabs, selected one, and went into the kitchen.

Rummaging through the storage shelves, he came upon a common kitchen solvent, dissolved some in half a glass of bottled water, and carried swab and glass to the writing table.

In the drawer there was good quality bond, on one sheet of which he penned an innocent letter to the Monocacy accommodation box. He blotted the ink and turned the sheet over.

Wetting the cotton tip, he twisted it into a fine point and very carefully began printing his report to Headquarters. When the sheet was covered it began to dimple, and he left it to dry naturally overnight.

In the morning he woke to the sound of trucks rumbling down the Paseo. He took a long soak in the tub, dressed, and walked stiffly to the writing table. Picking up the letter, he carried it to the kitchen, warmed an electric iron, and pressed the sheet smooth. The S/W system he had used was an emergency one and of low resistance to detection, but airmail bound for America was unlikely to be checked by Spanish censorship, even if spot censorship was in effect.

Having addressed an envelope, Peter sealed the letter inside and walked three blocks to the nearest post office, where he bought stamps. He did not deposit the letter there but continued down Alcalá and dropped it in the first *buzón*. Even if, against very long odds, the S/W message were detected, the lack of a return address made its origin untraceable.

It was Monday now, and he thought it unlikely that his report would reach Langley much before Wednesday afternoon.

At which time he would be in Gredos.

Stepping into a café, Peter stood at the bar and ate orange slices, then sweet bread and a tall glass of hot *café con leche* laced with strong brandy. Breakfast over, he took a taxi to the Puerta del Sol, got out, and walked along Calle Mayor until the stores began to open and he was able to buy ready-made clothing to replace most of what had been destroyed in the hotel. From there he went to a sporting goods shop, bought rubber waders, sweater, poplin jacket, creel, and spinning tackle, assuming the mountain wind would be too brisk for fly lines.

Back at his apartment he packed his bag and loaded the Mercedes. Then he took the La Coruña road out of Madrid, past the Escorial and the Valley of the Fallen, whose 500-foot stone cross he could see distantly through pines that bordered the roadway. Another twenty kilometers and he turned southwest toward Avila, whose ancient sand-colored walls never failed to arouse in him a sense of awe and respect. South then from Avila to Barraco, where he left the highway and headed west another hour, climbing the steep, winding road 6,000 feet through pine forests and melting snow to the Parador.

The lodge was constructed of native stone and laid out as a short-stemmed T; it was two stories where the ground was level and three on the sloping side, with a modified mansard roof and gabled windows. The sedge surrounding the lodge was still winter-brown, and the trees barely in bud. To the south stood the snowy Gredos range, and to the north, the Avila chain, whose blunt crests rubbed the coasting clouds.

As Peter stepped from the car's warm interior cold wind snapped his jacket. He lifted out his bag and tackle, and strode toward the stone-framed entrance. A bellboy came out to greet him, evoking a memory of young José Perdomo so brutally destroyed.

At the desk Peter confessed to not having wired for a reservation, but the manager said the lodge was only half filled and offered Peter a selection of rooms.

Peter chose a small suite with a stone fireplace and an

unobstructed view of the Gredos range ten or twelve miles away. There had been fighting there during the Civil War; but the country was difficult for offensive maneuvers, and the persistence of Republican defenders had delayed the Nationalist march on Madrid.

Through the manager Peter hired a fishing guide, a grizzled mountaineer of sixty named Eufemio who brought with him a landing net, a tackle box, and two *botas* of white wine.

By noon they were on the bank of the Tormes River, a narrow, clear stream whose icy flow was snow-fed like Bariloche's Traful. Eufemio laid the wine on the shallow bottom, made lure suggestions to Peter, and set about building a fire.

In three casts Peter hooked a brown trout that weighed five pounds gutted and landed a seven-pound salmon trout. He warmed his hands at the fire while Eufemio split the fish and grilled them on a *parilla* of peeled green branches.

There were bread and salt, and wine so cold that it made Peter's head throb, but the hot, flaky feast eaten with his fingers filled and satisfied his belly. He lay back on the cool ground and watched the scattered clouds while Eufemio knelt on the bank and trailed his hands in the water, occasionally pulling out a small, translucent crayfish, which he thrust into Peter's creel.

High, endlessly high, a SAC jet from Torrejón streaked its chalky contrail across the sky, speeding westward like a silver arrowhead, reminding Peter of his mission in Spain. With a sigh he sat up and drained the last mouthful of *blanco* from the leather bottle, reflecting that for nearly an hour he had been able to erase the blackboard of his mind and think of other things. Operationally he was immobilized, so there was no profit in fretting over inactivity; in due course he would return to Madrid and work the old leads while looking hard for new ones.

In the afternoon Peter trudged upward with Eufemio to a six-foot fall whose force had scooped out a deep pool in the river bed. Salmon leaped through the iridescent veil, and the guide hung a small crayfish on Peter's hook and pointed at the swirling water.

The bait was barely out of sight when a salmon struck, a ten-pounder that did battle for a quarter of an hour before turning belly up and drifing into the shallows where Eufemio waited with his net. Peter kept that one, and landed another dozen that he released. At four o'clock the wind quickened and shadows scudded over the mountainside, so the two men began the long descent, the gutted salmon in Peter's creel on a bed of mountain grass. At the Parador kitchen Peter asked the chef to prepare some of the salmon for his breakfast and the rest for dinner the following night.

With the guide he fished for another two days on the Tormes, visited a branch of the Alberche on the third day, and spent the fourth day climbing through the ibex preserve in the wild Gredos range.

That evening Peter studied his face in the mirror and noted that the stitch perforations had closed and that the sun and the wind had burned his face an even brown color.

He slept deeply and dreamlessly that night—as he had every night at the Parador—and after breakfast he loaded the Mercedes and drove back to Madrid.

After unpacking in his apartment he telephoned Fermín Hernández and learned from the detective that the hotel room stakeout had been unproductive. Hernández thanked him for his cooperation, speculated that they would never know who had planted the bomb, and wished Peter an uneventful stay in Spain henceforth.

From Espalter, Peter drove to Calle Eslava, parked near the Sainz home, and was admitted by one of the maids, still dressed in mourning black.

"The *condesa* told me I might continue to work in the professor's library," he said.

"*Sí*, it is so, *señor*. The *condesa* herself instructed me."

He went to the library, opened the door, and saw Marisa at the desk going through a thick file. She looked up quickly and said, "Oh, it's you, Dr. Ward. I had begun to wonder if you would return. From Portugal, I believe?"

TEN

"Lisbon," Peter said. "The Royal Library—and the University Library at Coimbra."

"Was your quest successful?"

"Reasonably." He walked toward her and saw that her eyes looked tired, her face drawn. "It was thoughtful of you to arrange the guest card for me."

"I hope you will make use of it." She looked down at the file.

"Did you go to your *finca*?"

"After the funeral, and I stayed until yesterday."

"The count—your father—is still there?"

She nodded slowly. "Everything is so unfamiliar to him

. . . as though he had never been there before. He has difficulty even in finding his way around our house."

"He went through a great deal."

Her face turned toward the window. "At night sometimes I hear him talking in his sleep—in Russian. He cries out and begs for mercy—they must have tortured him very cruelly."

Peter nodded. "It seems strange that after so many years they would set him free."

"Very strange—unless it is that he was of no further use to them. Perhaps his mind—" One hand lifted to her mouth and her eyes sparkled with tears.

"At least he is alive and in good health."

"Only half alive," she said tautly, "and he acts almost like a child." She dried her eyes with a small handkerchief. "His only pleasure is cutting trees."

Peter stared at her. "Cutting trees?"

She nodded forlornly. "With an axe—the work he did at Vorkuta. So long as he works he seems happy, but when I persuade him to stop he . . . he sits and stares out of the window. I—it is like not having a father, Doctor. I don't know what to do."

"Psychiatry?"

She shook her head slowly. "If it were learned that the count were undergoing psychiatric treatment our cause would be destroyed. '"

"You could take him to another country—Switzerland, for instance."

"And have questions asked about our leaving Spain? No. The rumors would be even worse." Her lips formed a thin line, and she glanced at the file she had been reading. "I hoped my father's old friends might be able to help, by visiting with him and slowly reminding him of the past, the years he lived in Spain—and bring back my mother's memory as well."

"He doesn't remember your mother?"

"He looked at a portrait of her and said he did not know who the *doña* was." Tears welled again in her eyes.

"And his old friends?"

"Dead," she said dully. "All dead."

"*All* of them?"

"Killed in the Civil or the Russian War; the others died natural or accidental deaths, or were assassinated." She gazed up at him. "Don Eduardo was the last."

"It seems impossible."

She gestured at the file, then closed it. "For my father the past does not exist; all that he remembers is work, hunger, and snow." Rising, she carried the file to the shelves, climbed a short ladder, and replaced it. "Our only visitors are

Paco and Don Felipe." She walked wearily to a chair and sat down.

Getting out his pipe, Peter filled and lighted it. When the tobacco was glowing he drew on it and said, "A close friend is a psychiatrist, *condesa*—"

"And in America," she murmured listlessly.

"No, in France. Lecturing at the University of Paris as an exchange professor. He planned to visit me in Spain and—"

Gripping the chair arms, she sat forward, and now her eyes were alive. "Could—*would* he be willing to see my father?"

"I'm sure he would."

Abruptly her face darkened. "It would be too much to hope that he speaks Spanish."

"He does," Peter said, and checked himself from adding, "as well as Russian." "I'll write today and ask him to come."

"That would be wonderful! He will stay at our *finca*, of course."

"Of course."

Rising, she said, "You do not know how happy you have made me, how hopeful I feel for the first time since my father returned." She spun around and her skirt flared. "I will always be grateful to you, Dr. Ward."

"Won't you call me Peter?"

"Peter." She flushed, smoothed her skirt, and averted her eyes.

"*Condesa*," Peter said quietly, "I know no one in Madrid. And I intend no irreverence to the memory of Don Eduardo by asking you to dine with me."

"To—tonight?"

"Tonight."

With a glance at the professor's empty chair she said, "Yes—with pleasure, and Don Eduardo will understand. After all, he devoted himself to making me happy." Pausing, she put a finger to her lips. "On the condition that after dinner we visit a flat where some friends of mine will be gathering to discuss life, the world, and Spanish politics. They form my *tertulia*, as we say in Spain. Perhaps you would find it interesting."

"I'm sure I will. I hadn't realized that politics was an active subject in Spain."

"Active—but discreet." Taking a deep breath, she looked down at her hands. "The return of my father frees me from so many things, Peter—so much formality, the requirement that I always conduct myself as an *infanta*—as if I really believed I would one day possess the throne of Spain."

"And you don't?"

She shook her head. "I never have—at least the realization

came to me when I returned to Spain and entered the university. There my eyes were opened to the facts of Spanish life, to how unsuitable would be another monarchy—and how minuscule were the chances of our Movement to gain the throne for one of our house." She broke off. "I surprise you."

"You do indeed."

She laughed uncertainly. "I suppose you thought of me as a *maja* in flowing eighteenth-century dress, modestly veiled, a black lace mantilla and high tortoise-shell comb in my hair?"

"Something like that—until I saw you." He sat in a chair. "Do Don Felipe and Paco know your true feelings?"

"Never! The Movement is their lives, and I could not bear to disillusion them. Besides, my father is now their matrix, their focal point. They look to him to lead them, and my role is one of assistant to my father who, for the present at least, needs me in a very real way."

Peter nodded. "Speaking of assistants, will Beatriz Peralta be returning?"

"Here?"

"Yes, the archives."

"I don't know," she said thoughtfully. "I have not seen her since the funeral. You met her here?"

"In a way. She was very close to Don Eduardo?"

"Close? He found her very helpful."

Peter's lips pursed. "Were they in any way . . . related?"

"What do you mean?"

"I'm not sure." Then, "Perhaps because of the way she was praying beside his casket."

"I—I don't care for Beatriz, I'm afraid. I never felt her to be—well, trustworthy."

"But she belonged to your Movement?"

"Many people are members." Her face hardened. "Even the man who killed Don Eduardo."

"I gathered that he and Beatriz were engaged."

Her eyebrows shot up. "She told you that?"

"Yes."

"Then perhaps it was so. Quite frankly I avoided her as much as I could. She was useful to Don Eduardo, doing typing and filing for him, and so I never voiced my objections." Her head slanted. "You were thinking she might be useful to you?"

"Not if you object to her."

"Well, she could find things for you in the files," she said doubtfully, "so employ her if you want."

"I'll discuss it with her," Peter said, "if I see her again."

Striding to the desk, Marisa picked up her gloves and

turned to him. "I must go now. At what hour will you call for me?"

"At whatever time is convenient."

"Nine, then. For a cocktail before going out."

Peter rose to take her hand. *"Hasta las nueve,"* she said, "and thank you for writing your friend."

"De nada." He bowed and saw her vanish through the doorway.

As he walked toward the desk he reflected that for all Marisa had said, Beatriz Peralta could still be the daughter of Professor Sainz. It would have been in character for Sainz not to have revealed the relationship to his young ward, and Peter could understand Beatriz's unwillingness to reveal her illegitimacy to a person of Marisa's position. And there was a further reason for an inconclusive verdict: as yet Peter could not judge the extent of Marisa's candor.

The opening to the count was sheer good fortune, he mused; the kind of operational break that so far had been lacking in his mission. Dr. Sol Podret was the ideal man to assess the count, and for all Peter knew, Sol might even be able to undam a part of the count's memory.

From the bookshelf he drew down the file Marisa had been studying, settled behind the desk and read it through, separating significant papers into a small pile as he went. The maid came in to ask if he cared for a drink of any kind—tea, coffee, *manzanilla*—and Peter told her he would be grateful for coffee.

Following her from the library, he went out to his car, unlocked the trunk, and took out a manila envelope, which he carried back to the desk. He waited until his coffee arrived before opening the envelope, and when the maid left he closed the door and moved the reading lamp to the center of the desk.

The envelope held fifty sheets of specially sensitized paper, and he laid a sheet over each of the typewritten sheets he had selected from the file, then pressed them together with the cover of a book and drew off a perfect copy. The chemistry of the process was complicated, but it related to photosensitivity and the special properties of carbon-content ink. The copies retained legible images for only a few days, but that was more than enough for his needs.

When he was finished he restored the original papers to the file and replaced it on the bookshelf, then fitted his copies into the envelope with the unused copying sheets.

For a time he sipped coffee, slowly pondering the paradoxical personalities of the public and the private *condesa*, and considering her mixed feelings over the count's return.

Initial joy over his survival must have given over to sorrow and a desperate desire to help restore his mind.

If you can do it, Sol, he said half aloud, you'll earn your pay for the next couple of years.

Then Peter closed the envelope, turned off the lamp, and went out to his car.

The townhouse of the Excelentísimos Señores Condes de Prados faced Calle Segovia, a few hundred yards south of the Royal Palace. What Peter could see of it in the darkness was Gothic Revival with iron-grilled lancet windows and a metal-shod oak door. He pulled the bell lever beside the door and heard it sound somewhere deep inside the building.

As he waited he reconstructed the two-part message he had transmitted to Headquarters asking for traces on the twenty-odd intimates of the Conde de Prados whom Marisa had described as being dead. If her information could be verified, it would lend added substance to his theory about the reason for Sainz's death. And though his request for Sol Podret by name might irritate some of Sol's colleagues, he had related it to the Headquarters suggestion he had received in Estoril, and specified Sol for his language capabilities.

Someone back at Headquarters would have to approve sending Sol to Spain. Avery Thorne never shied away from making decisions, but routine matters were decided at lower levels where the assumption of responsibility was not uniformly welcome.

The door opened on a frock-coated butler who said, *"¿Señor?"*

"Peter Ward. I believe the *condesa* is expecting me."

"Please come in."

Taking Peter's coat, he led him down a dimly lighted hall whose walls were hung with armorial trappings and tapestries, to a lighted room from which filtered the sound of voices. As the butler announced him, Peter saw Marisa sitting in a tall petit-point chair facing Paco Arastegui and Felipe Carbajal.

She rose and came to greet him, gave him her hand, and said, "I believe you know Colonel Arastegui and Don Felipe."

"We've met." He shook hands with the two men, and Arastegui said, "*Jerez* or something stronger?"

"Jerez."

Marisa said, "Were you able to find what you needed in the archives?"

Nodding, he took the sherry glass from El Tuerto and held it in his hand.

Carbajal said, "Not having Don Eduardo to guide you must present something of a handicap."

"It does, but fortunately I have ample time for my work."

Arastegui said, "We were discussing some matters affecting out Movement, Doctor." His manner was coolly correct and predictably lacking in warmth.

"Don't let me interrupt."

Carbajal glanced at Marisa, who said, "Since all of us lead rather insular lives, Dr. Ward might provide a somewhat broader view of our problem."

"The *only* problem, my dear," said Carbajal, "is your own stubbornness—if you will permit me the observation."

Looking at Marisa, Peter saw her mouth tighten. Arastegui said with obvious reluctance, "Briefly, we are trying to persuade the *condesa* of the need for quick and dramatic action. Don Felipe and I feel that already too much time has passed since the count's return. His followers—especially the men and women of the Brigadas—are clamoring for his appearance." He looked at Carbajal, who picked up the cue.

"Politically speaking, unless the count appears and stirs new fires among his partisans, he might as well not have returned."

"Which do you prefer, Don Felipe," Marisa rejoined, "a disastrous appearance or none at all?"

"It need not be 'disastrous,' as you put it," Carbajal bridled. "The count has only to stand at attention while the Brigadas march by. Surely there is no risk in that."

Glancing at Peter, she bit her lip. "How soon would the review take place?"

"As soon as possible," Carbajal said, and Arastegui nodded agreement.

"A month, then."

Carbajal shook his head, and the light darkened the liver spots on his face. "Much too far off," he declared. "Certainly no longer than a week from now." He turned to Arastegui. "Paco, you will need no more than a week to arrange everything?"

"Four days' time is sufficient, Don Felipe."

Silently Marisa considered their words. Then she said, "Tomorrow I will return to the *finca*, appraise my father's condition, and let you know my decision."

"Tomorrow," Carbajal said with a heavy sigh. "Very well, *condesa*, we will expect to hear from you then."

Arastegui moved toward her chair. "Consider, Marisa, how much depends on your decision." Then he took her hand and bowed, followed by Carbajal. The two men said good-night to Peter and left the room.

When Peter looked back at Marisa, her face was anguished. Rising, she distractedly mixed a whiskey and took a long drink.

Peter said, "Persuasive men."

"Very determined, no?" She drank again. "Now perhaps you understand my problem. Because the government has never interfered with our Movement, its members have developed a feeling of immunity. But even if my father were well I would not want him to make fiery speeches to the Brigadas. There is a limit to government tolerance, after all."

"Undoubtedly." Peter finished his sherry and mixed a short highball of Canadian Club.

"And what do you think of it all?" she asked.

"I think Carbajal's enthusiasm could lead to adventurism."

"In what way?"

Peter looked down at his glass. "Once 'new fires' are stirred in the Brigadas—as he put it—the fires will require continuous fueling."

"Go on."

"Demonstrations could become violent and—"

"Bloodshed would result," she finished. "Yes, you are entirely right. Perhaps I've been wrong in concealing my feelings so many years. This may well be the time when it would be better for everyone, my father included, to dissolve the Movement." Tilting her glass again, she drank, ran a hand lightly through her hair, and said, "I'm grateful for your views, Peter. You, at least, have no axe to grind, no personal interest in the outcome."

Her last sentence stung Peter, who said, "Well, as an American I'm interested in European political stability."

She smiled a little cynically. "Meaning your SAC and naval bases in Spain."

Finishing his highball, Peter set the empty glass on a tray. "To bring up a more pleasant subject, how did you pass the afternoon?"

"Very likely you won't believe me," she said quietly, "but after I left you I scrubbed floors and took care of two sick children whose mother was working in a factory."

"The Condesa de Prados?"

She shook her head. "Marisa Pérez, *señor*. Titles echo harshly from the walls of the poor. I help the nuns as I can, Peter."

"Noblesse oblige."

She shrugged. "I hope that one day the word aristocrat will become less obscene among working people."

"Are there many like you?"

"Too few, I'm afraid."

"Then you deserve the finest dinner in Madrid."

"The Jockey?"

He nodded, but Marisa shook her head. "Peter, I'd really prefer some less conspicuous place. Will you trust my choice?"

"Of course."

Following her into the hall, he helped her into a lightweight black coat, and when they were seated in the Mercedes she said, "Drive down Bailén as far as Calle de Toledo."

"And . . . ?"

"The restaurant is called El Hongo," she said, and laughed. "In English there could never possibly be a restaurant named The Mushroom."

"Never," he agreed. He slid the car into gear and followed her directions until they pulled up before a doorway whose weathered sign bore the restaurant's name in flaked letters.

Locking the Mercedes, Peter walked down the entrance stairway that gave out into a single medium-sized room with a large stone fireplace and perhaps twenty neatly set tables. At the far end a couple sat drinking at a small bar. No more than three tables were occupied by early diners.

"It isn't the Jockey Club," Marisa whispered, "but I'm fond of it. I began coming here while I was still in the university."

A fat, dark-haired woman in a starched apron waddled toward Marisa, gave her an *abrazo,* and said, "Señorita Marisa—it is so long since you have come here. Have you been well?"

"Quite well," she said, and turned to Peter. "Dr. Ward, la Señora de Céspedes."

"Encantado," Peter said.

"Igualmente, Señor Doctor." With one hand she gestured at the empty tables. "You may have any table you desire."

"By the fireplace?" Marisa asked.

"Even without a fire?"

"Even so, *señora."*

After the first drink had come, Marisa lifted her glass and touched it to Peter's. They drank together and her eyes locked with his. "Now you may tell me," she said calmly, "who you really are and what you are doing in Spain."

ELEVEN

"Who I—?" Peter began, broke off, and drank again—a long drink that gave him time to recover from the thrust of her question. "Are you serious?" he said warily.

"Quite serious." She took a cigarette from a gold-washed case and allowed him to light it. "Paco made inquiries about you at your embassy. It seems you were once in the diplomatic service."

"True."

"At your embassy in Buenos Aires, among other posts."

Peter nodded. For the moment it was safer to let her continue.

"A distant cousin of Paco's was Spanish ambassador in Argentina when you were there."

Peter's eyes narrowed as he glanced at the ceiling trying to recall the ambassador's name. "Gomuza?" he tried. "The Marqués of—"

"Gamazo," she supplied.

"Of course. A short, balding little man, but very shrewd and awfully well connected in Buenos Aires."

Marisa nodded. "He remembered you, Peter. You played polo on an Argentine team, he said, and left Buenos Aires rather suddenly."

"Suddenly?"

"I believe it had to do with a Russian diplomat who was declared *persona non grata* by the Argentine government."

"Oh yes," Peter said vaguely. "He applied at our embassy for asylum and the ambassador asked me to escort him to Washington."

"I see." Lifting her glass, she drank, and Peter hoped the interrogation was at an end. There had been a little more to Porenkov's defection than a simple request for asylum, but the Spanish ambassador could never have known the details.

"Why you?" she asked. "Were you the embassy security officer?"

He shook his head. "At that time I spoke a little Russian. The thought was that the gentleman's nerves might be soothed if he could speak his native tongue during the flight. It took nineteen hours in those pre-jet days, Marisa."

Her eyes twinkled. "You kept him soothed all those hours?"

Peter chuckled. "He kept himself loaded. After all, the drinks were free. And more than a few people speak Russian, Marisa—including you."

Her eyebrows shot up. "Who told you that?"

"Don Eduardo."

The immediate danger had passed, he judged, but to dispel any lingering doubts he told her of his wife's death and his subsequent return to the practice of law, of the Blackstone Foundation grant, and what he hoped to accomplish with its help.

She did not return to the subject, and after they had ordered he asked about her life and learned that she liked riding, shooting, skiing, and painted landscape oils at her *finca*. She had been educated in Switzerland, England, and Spain, and ached for the day when she could take up legal battle in the Spanish courts to gain broader rights for Spanish women.

"Why not now?" he asked.

"Now? Don Felipe would find it unseemly in his *infanta*. Please, a little more *rojo*, if you will."

Her glass refilled, she said, "I still find it hard to think of you as scholarly."

"Why?"

"Because you look much more the man of action. And you're very, very subtle. Without your glasses you're rather handsome, you know. Is that why you wear them so seldom?"

"Only for reading." Peter sighed and thought that in the history of the international feminist movement no advocate had been as lovely or as intelligent as this reluctant young *condesa*. Wine was dissolving the ramparts of royal reserve, and he noticed that when she smiled her cheeks displayed a pair of sinful dimples.

Lifting her glass, she murmured, "We call red wine the tears of Spain."

"A sober thought."

"But appropriate to our san—sanguin—our *bloody* history," she finished. "Oh, Peter, I'm so tired of responsibility, so dreadfully weary of pretending to be what I'm not. All I want is to stay at the *finca* and care for my father, or what is left of him. The intrigues—this impossible scheme to capture the throne . . ." Her voice trailed away. Unsteadily she dried moist eyes and lifted her glass. "Let's have another—to follow the other."

"*Prosit*."

Their first course arrived, and as they ate her mood leveled off from the extremes of gaiety and moroseness. She was a good companion again, but conversely, from Peter's professional point of view, a less interesting conversationalist. At midnight a small orchestra arrived, and they danced a few times before Marisa suggested that they leave.

Paying the check, Peter left a healthy tip for the waiter, said good-night to the proprietress, and promised to return. They got into the Mercedes, and as he started the engine she said, "I hope you won't be shocked by my friends."

"Shocked?"

"Well—disapprove of them. You're so proper and they're so—well, unconventional is almost euphemistic."

Peter grinned in the darkness. Proper, indeed. "I'm no Henry Adams abroad," he said, restraining a chuckle. "If I get out of line, tell me."

"I shall."

The place she took him to was a peaked loft atop an old apartment building on Zurbarán. Its floor space was unobstructed by partitions, and over the years considerable expense had been spared in maintaining the floor, walls, and plumbing. A dozen or so thick candles shed soft light around the atelier, whose dusty skylight framed a hazy moon.

Their host was a lean young man who wore a black beard and a paint-stained blue work shirt. His name was Eddy Valenoía, and he was clearly sorry to have an American on his premises. Josefina—his *amiga,* as Marisa tactfully described her—was no more than seventeen or eighteen, taller than Eddy, white of face, and slim and graceful as a lynx in pink shirt and tight blue jeans that contoured her buttocks provocatively. Smiling a soft, secretive smile, she clung so closely to Eddy as to suggest an emanation of ectoplasm from a medium. Peter scanned a row of the atelier's many oil paintings and realized that Josefina had posed for at least half of them, among which were several striking nudes.

Around the big studio couples lounged on mattresses, ottomans, and boxes; the air held the scent of coffee and brandy; and the *ambiente* was warmly voluptuous. Marisa led him around, introducing him to students, graduates, artists, ballerinas, *chicos de bien,* a political-science instructor bearded and eczematous, a pair of Basque dykes whose butch half smoked a small meerschaum pipe, a choreographer and his catamite. . . . Names were uttered and drifted away like smoke. To Peter, it seemed as if everyone was there except Willie the Sculptor. Someone handed them coffee from a dented brass samovar and pointed out a brandy bottle on the floor. Its aroma was as harsh as raw *caña* and Peter declined, though Marisa added some to her coffee.

They found space against the wall. Marisa put her cup

on the floor and stretched her arms and arched her body in catlike pleasure. "I love just being here," she murmured with half-closed eyes. "It's a refuge for me, a place of escape —my contact with the world of reality, the real Spain."

Peter sipped his unsweetened coffee. "The real Spain?"

"The Spain of tomorrow—*my* Spain."

Peter smothered a smile. "Social justice, freedom, and egalitarianism?"

"Yes—all that and more. Much more, Peter." Her eyes were open now, wide and serious. "No fixed extremes of wealth and poverty. No poverty at all, and no class hatreds."

"You might make a good queen at that."

Her head tilted regally. "Don't jest. You know I have no such aspirations or desires. I want evolution in our political process, not revolution."

"Ah, that others might hear you," he sighed.

"Others?"

"The Jacobin fringe in my own country."

A man eased over to Marisa and engaged her in conversation. He was followed by a stern-faced girl in thick glasses. Others came and left; some stayed. Peter glanced toward the skylight and saw a heavy veil of tobacco smoke. The prewar rent-raising parties in Greenwich Village must have resembled this gathering, he reflected, with its assortment of idealists, impracticalists, free-love (until the first pregnancy) advocates, revolutionaries, creative spirits, and poseurs. Marisa added the Foxcroft, Park Avenue element before which the unwashed could grovel enjoyably, and her reward was self-identification with their diverse causes and a feeling of indulging in things *verboten*.

Peter studied her relaxed features, her youthful eyes and quizzical mouth, and decided that her innate intelligence and sense of order would restrain her from ideological or other excess.

Yawning, he looked covertly at his wristwatch and saw that the hour was nearly two, but Marisa was talking animatedly to a group of sprawled forms and gave no sign of fatigue.

Some of the candles had burned their length, and with the constant influx and outflow of guests he had lost track of who was in the studio and who had left. The brandy bottle and two successors were long empty and there had been no coffee for nearly an hour. Peter yawned again, sought a comfortable position against the sloping wall, and folded his arms.

From one corner came the sound of a guitar, and in the dim light Peter made out Josefina lying on the floor in close embrace with someone other than the host.

The scene reminded him of an off-campus apartment he and a half-dozen classmates had inherited in their senior year. In an ancient frame building at the foot of College Hill, the place held the dust and red plush furnishings of the 1870's, and its bizarre features had proved a lodestone for pretties from Boston, Wellesley Hills, and Hamp. There had been considerable drinking and *amour*, he recalled, but all in good humor and with a certain amount of flair. On graduation, he and his fellow conspirators awarded the keys to another group of blades in a tradition three-quarters of a century old.

"Peter! You're falling asleep!"

Blinking, he stirred himself and focused half-open eyes on Marisa's laughing face. "You are old, father Peter, the young girl said," Peter parodied.

"Yet your walk is exceedingly lithe," she improvised. "It *is* late, isn't it? Shall we go?"

Patting the back of his hand, she rose to her knees and said good-bye to her listeners. Eddy was lecturing to the lesbians on a chartreuse-vermilion oil, and as he stepped over prone bodies, Peter suggested to Marisa that they not disturb him.

She took his arm, waved at several of the still-conscious guests, and gave her hand to Josefina, who had scrambled to her feet, hastily tucked in her shirttails, and joined them. As Peter thanked the girl he noticed for the first time a thin gap between her two upper incisors—the legendary Mark of Venus. *Gat-tothed was she, soothly for to seye*, he dredged from the well of memory, and was grasping for the rest when a cigarette lighter briefly outlined the faces of a couple seated in a dark corner. Peter felt his face freeze, then the light went out and he forced himself to turn toward Marisa. "Come along, Peter," she coaxed. "Fresh air will do you good."

"A world of good," he muttered. He took her arm and opened the door without looking back.

As he drove through the quiet streets toward Calle Segovia, she said, "Why don't you come to the *finca* with me tomorrow?"

"I think I ought to wait to hear from my Paris friend."

"Yes—yes, I'd forgotten about him." For a few moments she was silent. Then: "For the last few hours I haven't thought about any of my troubles, Peter. I—it's good to live outside yourself when you can."

"Essential," he agreed, and said nothing more until he braked the Mercedes beside the curb in front of the Prados home.

Then, walking with her to the recessed portals, he thanked her for an unusual evening.

"I'm glad you liked it, Peter. I know I did." Turning toward him she lifted her eyes to his, and in that moment she seemed achingly desirable . . . and terribly young.

When he made no move she said, "I thought in America couples always kissed on their first date."

"Not always," he said huskily, "and hardly ever if the girl happens to be a countess." But bending over, he kissed her forehead at the hairline.

"No . . ." she murmured. She stood on tiptoe and put her arms around his shoulders. Inexpertly her lips met his and pressed them warmly. "Like that," she whispered and stepped back. "I'm a woman, Peter—not a political party."

"I—" he began awkwardly, swallowed, and began again. "Marisa, I'm much older than you."

"And—?" she challenged.

He swallowed again. "Technically—biologically, I mean, I'm old enough to be your father."

"But you aren't my father," she said throatily, and kissed the tip of his chin. "And you're much younger than any number of the nobility who would like to marry me."

Peter shook his head. "That lets me out. Morganatic marriages aren't notably successful."

"I'd say it depends upon the couple involved."

"Granted. Particularly the state of the consort's morale." He became serious. "I'll let you know when I've heard from my friend in Paris."

"I'll be hoping and praying."

"Marisa, what decision are you going to give Carbajal tomorrow?"

"Tomorrow? None at all. Not until I've heard from you. You do agree that it's wise to postpone my father's appearance?"

"Wholeheartedly," he said, and walked back to his car.

He sat in the darkness, his car engine idling, until the front door opened and closed behind her. Then he shoved the car into gear and drove slowly away.

Had it not been for the illumination of the lighter flame in the studio corner he would have taken time now to ponder the two dissimilar persons in Marisa Pérez and their significance to the Royalist Movement. Instead, he visualized again the two faces he had glimpsed so briefly in the darkness: the young woman's oval face, her concave cheeks; the constrasting swarthy complexion of the older man beside her, his rounded semi-Oriental face and close-cropped hair.

The woman was Beatriz Peralta, who had exchanged deep mourning for the diversions of the *tertulia*. The man—from his brief, radioed description—could well be the Soviet officer missing from Teheran: Colonel Sergei N. Volkov of the GRU.

TWELVE

If the assets and resources of the Madrid station were at his disposal, Peter mused, he would have surveillance personnel swarming over the old building in Calle Zurbarán, identifying Eddy's remaining guests by name, date, and place of birth, with alternating teams reserved for tracking Volkov and Beatriz Peralta to their joint or separate lairs.

That was exploiting operational leads by the book.

But even with Squirrel humming its electronic song, the data and conclusions it could produce were useless without the local application of human eyes, brains, and limbs, and Peter was strongly tempted to violate his own security restrictions and contact the Madrid COS to lay the problem on the line. But in doing so he would be tacitly admitting that the ramifications of his mission exceeded his capacity to monitor and control.

So, he decided, for the present he would remain isolated from the station and play the expanding case as best he could.

Besides, he could not actually identify Beatriz's escort as Volkov, and Headquarters had not positively notified him that Volkov was in Madrid—sans moustache. Grasping this rationale, Peter turned back toward Zurbarán, the thought crossing his mind that Beatriz might have seen him just as he had noticed her.

If she had, there was the further question of what significance she would attach to his appearance at Eddy's. He had obviously been there as Marisa's escort, so unless Beatriz knew of his CIA connection she might not mention it to Volkov—the *possible* Volkov, Peter corrected quickly.

But first there had been the matter of the planted Communist communiqué and later the attempt on his life by a booby trap of his bed, so it was apparent that someone resented his appearance in Madrid.

And even if her escort *was* Volkov, you could not instantly assume, Peter reasoned, that Beatriz Peralta was aware of his line of work. Public juxtaposition of a Soviet intelligence officer and one of his agents was almost unheard of.

There were areas of the world where the Sovs did so in the belief that the local counterintelligence services were beneath contempt, but Europe was not one of them.

Still, assuming that what Thorne and Hopwood had told him was true, then the Spanish Service—the DSN—had lost its once-sharp edge, and the RIS would quickly react to changed and more favorable circumstances. And an old hand like Volkov, in any case, could be expected to disregard certain conspiratorial rules.

Hell, Peter thought, even I do.

Turning onto Zurbarán, he looked at his watch and saw that twenty-three minutes had elapsed since he and Marisa had left Eddy's atelier. Twenty-three minutes was time enough to loft a missile from Khabarovsk to Offut Field; time enough to fly a fighter mission and get back to the wardroom cribbage board. It was also time enough for Beatriz and her pal to have cut the scene, dusted, disappeared into the matrix of a city with 2 million inhabitants.

Parking half a block from the apartment building, Peter turned off the headlights and slouched down behind the steering wheel. A street light only a few yards from the entrance cast a diffused glow over the vacant sidewalk, and Peter hoped it might be enough to distinguish faces by. A source-light scanner would be a handy item, he reflected, but none was within several hundred miles, and so, like the castaway who found himself without matches, he excused himself on the grounds that he had not anticipated needing one when he started the trip.

By craning his neck he could see the studio windows atop the building, barely defined by the remaining candle flames. And so long as there was light, he decided, there would be guests on the premises.

He lighted his pipe, shielding the match behind the door panel, and recalled that he had always loathed stationary surveillance for its shackling inactivity. The aroma of Middleton 5 gave him a feeling of creature comfort as he stared into the night. Smoking was something to do, and his mind's built-in alarms had never yet allowed him to fall asleep while he held a pipe between his teeth.

A couple left the entrance and turned away from the light, but as he peered at their receding backs he knew that their relative heights eliminated them as his quarry. A few minutes later the guitarist staggered out, guitar slung over his back; then it was a quarter of an hour before the next couple emerged. The Basque dykes this time, arms closely linked as they hurried off into the night. Taking the pipe from his mouth, he grunted in distaste and set about filling the empty bowl.

The Norwegian exchange student was the next departure, his unkempt blond hair making identification easy.

Then, for no logical reason, Peter thought of Don Felipe Carbajal, *impulsor* of the Movement. An aging Silenus, he mused, subtle and insinuating as Pandarus. Carbajal, on whom Squirrel had reported NDI—No Derogatory Information. Neither a clean bill of health nor cause for particular alarm. Carbajal had a vested interest in keeping the Movement moving, so his pressure on Marisa was as understandable as El Tuerto's. From their point of view they either had to capitalize on the count's return or see their following drift away disillusioned and disgusted. The prolonged passivity of a *status quo* situation soured even true believers, however wild their dream.

The vision of thrones, power, and riches, he thought moodily, had corrupted clerics and kings—and destroyed them in the end.

Guests were trailing out now in twos and threes, and Peter blinked smarting eyes as he strained to make out their forms and faces. This must be the last of them, he told himself, as they parted company under the streetlight and moved off in different directions.

Still no Señorita Peralta, with or without friend.

Grumpily he sucked on his dead pipe, then as an afterthought peered up at Eddy's windows. They were invisible now, even their frames blending with the darkness of the roof. The candles had gone out.

It was possible that his targets were sleeping in the dark loft, but Peter felt the odds were against it. Still, to hedge his bet he lingered another five minutes, then accepted the conclusion that Beatriz and her escort had left Eddy's before he had returned from Marisa's home.

In a black humor, Peter started the engine, raced it irritably, and drove past the long-watched entrance without a further glance. At the intersection he turned on his headlights and swung the Mercedes down the Paseo de la Castellana, past the Columbus statue and the dark façade of the Museo del Prado, to Espalter and the welcome sight of the apartment garage.

Groggily he rode the lift to his floor, and when he was getting into bed he looked at his watch and saw that the time was a quarter after four. Late enough for anyone, he growled, and too damn late for me.

Then his mind drafted a radio message to Headquarters, and recast it twice; but in the end he decided to send nothing at all.

Half asleep, he remembered his parting from Marisa, and thought how many years it had been since he had kissed or

been caressed by a girl so astonishingly and sweetly innocent.
And how poignant the moment had been.

Arriving at the Sainz home in mid-morning, Peter was admitted by the maid and went directly to the library. He searched the desk until he came across the professor's address book, and opened it to the letter P. The page contained numerous Spanish names, but not the name Peralta. Frowning, he went through the rest of the entries in the book until he found the address of Felipe Carbajal and copied it on his memo pad. The preceding page listed a Bartolomé, Pedro; a Bezúcar, Amelia, and the name Beatriz.

Peter added her address and telephone number to his memo pad, returned it to his coat, and as an afterthought pocketed the address book for possible future use.

The maid brought in coffee, and as he drank it he thought of Marisa on her way to the *finca,* and commended her wisdom in temporizing with Carbajal's demands. Then he took the morning paper from the coffee tray and scanned its uniformly drab front page, halting to read a dispatch from Rome headed: *Resurgence of Spanish Royalist Movement.*

The byline was that of *ABC*'s Rome correspondent, who quoted an *Il Paese* story to the effect that the return of Rodrigo, Count of Prados (from where was left unspecified), might spark a dramatic change in the lugubrious Spanish political scene. *Il Paese* estimated the count's adherents at 150,000 active and militant reactionaries, and the Brigadas at 45,000 well-trained paramilitary troops. The Italian paper, according to the dispatch, went on to say that tens of thousands of uninformed Spaniards might rally to the Royalist cause out of disgust with Franco's Fascist regime, and warned Italians that Spanish Royalism was as much to be feared as the discredited Italian brand. Peter laid the paper on the desk, and turned to gaze out over the ill-kept garden below. *Il Paese* was a notorious pro-Communist organ that frequently served the Soviets as a means of launching some devious and covert operation whose effect might not be noticed for as long as a year. *Il Paese* was also a useful medium with which to smear and assassinate the characters not only of Italian anti-Communists, but those in other countries whom the Kremlin deemed dangerous. The Arab press was always quick to reprint sensational stories originating in *Il Paese*, as were the newspapers of emerging Africa and South America—particularly Uruguay and Argentina with their large Italian populations.

So while politically sophisticated readers in Europe were not likely to be misled by *Il Paese,* millions of non-Continental readers were.

To Peter it was less surprising that *Il Paese* had fired the initial shot than that the government-controlled press of Spain had echoed its reverberation. Political criticism was normally as absent from the pages of Spanish newspapers as anticlerical themes, and so Peter deduced that the government had been disturbed by the *Il Paese* article and had reacted by authorizing its reprint—either as a tacit warning to Spanish citizens or to the Royalists themselves.

As an augury it was negative, but to Peter it represented tangible evidence of Soviet interest in the Royalists. Added to the possible presence in Spain of Colonel Sergei Volkov, the *Il Paese* plant gave additional weight to Avery Thorne's original theory.

The maneuver left Peter with a feeling of frustration, since the Soviet goal could not yet be clearly defined. A continuing objective of the Soviets was to establish diplomatic relations with Spain, thus gaining an embassy sanctuary in Madrid from which they could not only control the clandestine Communist party of Spain, but could spread subversion throughout Spain and into Portugal, and from there to Portuguese Africa, where they were already heavily committed.

One interpretation, Peter mused, was that the Kremlin regarded the Royalists as even more hostile to the establishment of a Soviet embassy in Spain than was Franco himself, and had begun a campaign to neutralize the Royalist Movement by compromising it with the current regime and discrediting it with the Spanish people. For years the Royalists had freely met and schemed only through the tolerance of Franco, and if that tolerance was replaced by a new and harder attitude, the Movement could not long survive.

Sucking in a deep breath, he decided to leave further analysis to Headquarters experts and to get on with his own immediate concerns. He dialed the apartment of Beatriz Peralta, but after eight unanswered rings he hung up and began a methodical search of the bookshelves for a history of the Prados family. The search took him well over an hour and ended in failure. As an afterthought he went through the stacked papers on the desk, and found what he sought in a worn, leather-bound volume whose cover was embossed with the Prados escutcheon.

Opening the book, he learned that the title had been created in the twelfth century by the king of Aragón to reward the bravery and loyalty of a knight who distinguished himself in the Second Crusade to the Holy Land. Over succeeding centuries, male heirs accompanied Cortez and Pizarro, married into houses of the Hapsburg and Bourbon, and demonstrated a faculty for being on the winning side.

Peter was so absorbed in the intricate chart that he was barely aware of someone entering the library, and subconsciously assumed that the maid had come to remove the tray. Then a voice said, "Dr. Ward—*buenos días.*"

Looking up, he saw Beatriz Peralta walking toward him.

"Buenos días," he said, and laid the book aside. "I telephoned you earlier."

"You telephoned me? Why?"

"To ask whether you could continue working here as my assistant—remember? Your familiarity with the filing system would save me a great deal of time."

Her eyes narrowed. "I—I'm afraid I cannot. I find that this room—this house—has too many memories for me now. Tragic memories."

"I understand. Last night I saw you as we were leaving Eddy's studio."

"Oh? I—we were there, and I saw Marisa but not you." She came closer to the desk and glanced at it nervously. "The person with me was Klaus Ehrlich, a German. He has an office in Madrid, and I am thinking of working for him as his secretary."

"It will be a change," Peter said. "Perhaps the work will be more interesting."

Her eyes were fixed on the book Peter had been reading. "Yes, a change. Did you mention to Marisa that you knew me?"

He shook his head, and her face relaxed as she said, "I came here to get something for Don Felipe."

"Carbajal?"

"Yes. That book—the Prados history."

Picking up the book, Peter held it toward her, then drew it back. "On second thought I'll finish it, Beatriz, and deliver it to Don Felipe."

"But he is waiting for it now." Her hand shot out. "Please give the book to me."

"It isn't available."

"Not—how can you say that? It was my father's book; now it is mine."

Peter shook his head. "Don Eduardo left everything to the *condesa.* And I have her authority to work here."

She bit her lip and gazed at him, her cheeks flushed with anger.

"Don't be upset," Peter said calmly. "I'll get the book to Carbajal."

Spinning around, she strode from the library, and Peter heard her open the front door and slam it shut.

Very interesting, he said half aloud, opened the book at his place, and continued reading.

By three o'clock he was back in his apartment, tuning the radio receiver to Headquarters' scheduled transmission. It came via the same jocular voice as before, informing him that every one of the men whose names Peter had queried was dead. In the last three years, four had died in accidents and one had apparently committed suicide.

The second part of the message told him that Dr. Podret was flying to Paris and would reach Madrid the following day.

As the repeat began Peter turned off the receiver and erased the tape recording. He lighted his pipe and reflected that no living Spaniard could either identify the Count of Prados from past association or denounce him as an impostor. And if he was the latter, he had been sent on his mission only after long and careful preparation by the RIS, with all the attention to detail so customary in a Soviet operation.

He called Carbajal's residence and learned that Don Felipe was not expected until late that night. Opening the Prados lineage book, he applied sensitized paper to the last two pages, then locked the copies, together with his transmitter/recorder, in the wall safe.

It was *siesta* time in Spain. Closing the bedroom blinds, Peter told himself that the presence in Madrid of Dr. Sol Podret was no longer an operational embellishment but an urgent necessity.

Part III

His day had begun with a walk through the vineyards, then breakfast in the patio with thrushes singing in the almond trees. To walk the warm, hard earth was pleasurable; his boots scuffed yellow dust, not powdery snow.

And the trees, he thought—trees so short as to seem almost stunted. Cork oaks in orchards and gnarled ancients over the countryside; locust trees and pines on the sloping foothills of the Alcubierre range, forests that thickened toward the nourishing Ebro, and everywhere a landscape of baked earth, jutting rock, and sun.

He had ridden to the river's edge, and while his horse drank he studied white clouds in the clear blue Catalonian sky, then followed a fence beyond which cattle grazed on rich spring grass. He repeated to himself that this was his land, his earth, the sky and mountains of his youth, and saw with remembered affection patches of romero *that fastened and grew on outcroppings until by mid-summer the rocks were blanketed by velvety lavender flowers.*

It was early one April in his long-forgotten life that

Yagüe had crossed the Ebro and beaten back the defenders of Lérida; later in the month battle lines had moved across the Prados finca, *leaving dead men and beasts, a shell-shot house and gutted chapel, its ancient cross pulled to the ground.*

Scars were still to be seen where newer brick had replaced the old; the original well had been filled with rock, sealed, and a new one dug. Of the corpses in that first well he might have known a man or two, and now he was the guardian of their common tomb.

The country was better than Madrid; better for its infinite, unmeasured spaces; for its unobstructed sun and peaceful nights; for the sea wind that slaked the cultivated earth.

And now as he sat in the dusk of the patio he drank sangría *and saw the swallows swarming overhead. They came each evening at nightfall, creatures of season and habit like himself, and he took pleasure from their quick and darting flight, remembering how as a boy he had lain on a grass-sweet hillside and tried to count them as they sped in from the sea.*

His hands and face were tanned the color of cork, and the dry air had nearly rid him of his once-convulsing cough. And each day another veil seemed to lift from his mind so that he could see a week, a month, deeper into the hidden past.

But the old man who had come to him was no one he had known before in this or any other country—the old man with his corsair face and mottled skin who addressed him as Excelentísimo Señor Conde. He had listened carefully to what the old man had to say because he spoke of marching troops and homage due and of the part he was required to play.

Fumbling for his makhorka *pouch, he remembered that it was in his room and that there was no need to seek a scrap of paper before he could smoke, because in his shirt pocket were cigarettes finer than even the guards could buy; cigarettes that yielded cool and savory smoke that satisfied his mouth and throat.*

And as he gazed at the ruby glow he remembered how close he had been to agreeing with Don Felipe when the girl —María Luisa—had arrived and argued furiously with the old man. So Don Felipe had gone back to Madrid, and now there was peace within the finca, *and overhead the last of the* golondrinas *fled the darkening sky.*

He smoked and listened to the distant sound of cattle, the horses nickering in the stables, and after a while she came out to sit with him and talk until it was time to go in for dinner.

THIRTEEN

When Dr. Sol Podret reached Peter's apartment it was mid-afternoon; he unpacked and took a shower, and as Peter handed him a drink he said, "I appreciate the name request, Peter. You know how to get things done."

"Headquarters hasn't changed." He gestured Podret into a chair and briefed him for the next hour.

When Peter finished, Sol got up and freshened his drink. "Curiouser and curiouser," he said moodily. "If Subject isn't the count, who is he?"

"That's your field, Sol."

The psychiatrist grunted. "At least you've provided access to the patient; some operators expect me to get one on the couch without as much as an introduction." His tongue made a sucking noise against his front teeth. "Whether he's amnesiac or not, Subject has had a series of traumatic experiences: the Civil War, the Russian front, and all those years of marginal survival. The facial scar fits, you say, and the scar itself—or rather the circumstances that produced it—could have been enough to stun his mind." Turning, he looked at Peter. "I don't hear you saying much."

"I've had my say. Rattle your gourd."

"Well, if we knew he had battle trauma we could simulate the environment and sounds of battle and see how he reacts." Podret took a small cigar from his pocket, bit off one end, and lighted the other. "From the experiences of our own men in Korea, Cuba, China, and Russia, we know considerable about the Soviet method of destroying men's will—reducing them to soulless, volitionless obedience. No sinister drugs are employed, nothing but a system carefully calculated to thwart and degrade all human instincts while exploiting every human weakness. Not surprisingly, the system succeeds."

"They've had half a century's raw material to experiment with."

Nodding, Podret blew smoke toward the ceiling. "Take the *sobatschnik*, Peter, the so-called kennel. Stripped naked, a prisoner is forced into this hutch measuring a yard by a yard by two feet wide and kept there at horribly cold or brutally hot temperatures. He's shamed by his nakedness, revolted by the stench of his own excreta. In isolation and complete silence he loses track of time, no matter what timekeeping formula he attempts. When he dozes he's taken out and forced to stand for hours in a comparatively luxurious room, and questioned by a well-dressed, fastidious interrogator. The contrast of his personal filth and nakedness shames and degrades the prisoner even more. Then he's hauled back to the *sobatschnik* and starved for a week, or perhaps they withhold water and he attempts to drink his own urine while guards jeer and revile him. Or his air holes are covered and he gets barely enough oxygen to sustain life—brain damage often results. Through all this he never knows when the next interrogation will come, and despite the horrors of the present, the uncertainties of the future prey on his mind—particularly if he has a family."

Podret shook his head. "He'll sign anything, agree to anything, Peter, because he's been gutted—*destripado*—by what he's gone through. The masters of the system regard it as impersonally as a fish-canning factory; meat arrives and is processed according to established assembly-line routine. What emerges is crated and shipped away, and they're ready for the next load. No man can escape transformation except through death."

"Transmogrification," Peter remarked.

"Better yet. You liberal-arts men have the advantage over us devotees of pure science."

"According to Kowalski it still goes on. The post-Stalin reforms—"

"Were quantitative rather than qualitative," Podret interrupted. "Meaning that somewhat fewer offenses are subject to the kind of processing I've described."

"Processing?"

Podret shrugged. "They don't regard it as punishment per se—it's a confession-producing mill. Then, with a confession in hand, the judge pronounces sentence. And in the U.S.S.R. . . . a lawyer is an officer of the court in every sense of the word—he's the prosecutor's assistant, not a defender as we know the term."

"And punishment is measured in terms of so many years in the *siblags*."

"Exactly. Where infractions are penalized by confinement in *vouros*—small, unheated huts where a man's nose, hands, and feet can turn to ice at fifty below zero." Shivering, Podret chafed his hands. "I have to assume that our subject went through everything I've described—all that plus twenty years of 'correctional labor.' See what we're up against?"

Peter nodded. "And all we're sure of is that every person

who knew him really well prior to nineteen forty-one is no longer among the living."

Podret frowned. "What about the last guy—Sainz?"

"According to the newspapers, the man who ran him down was dead before his car ever went over the cliff—skull crushed with a hard, tubular object."

"Like an iron pipe?" Podret muttered, and began to pace the room. He was shorter than Peter, balding and with a sallow skin. Even when clean-shaven his face was shadowed by his beard.

Peter got up from his chair and knocked ashes from his pipe. "They're expecting you at the *finca* tonight, Sol."

"So I get not even a night to wallow in the stews of old Madrid," he complained. "What about you?"

"I'll join you tomorrow or the next day."

"How do I get there?"

"Take my Mercedes."

"A *Mercedes?*"

"It's a five-hour drive, Sol. Four hundred eighty kilometers or thereabouts."

"Okay—but why a Mercedes?"

Peter shrugged. "Car calculated most likely to inflame the natives." From the table he lifted a Shell road map of Spain and handed it to the doctor. "Highway eleven to Guadalajara, Zaragoza, and Lérida; then south toward Borjas another twelve kilometers. If you can't find the entrance ask any peasant—the Prados estate covers most of the land between Lérida and Borjas."

"Sure you don't want to go with me?"

"I've got things to do in Madrid."

Podret laughed shortly. "From what you've told me, Peter, I'd judge one of the principal things is just staying alive."

"Some days are more trying than others," he conceded. "Want me to confirm your arrival?"

"Not unless you're transmitting something important. If they can't trust me to get to Madrid from Paris they'd better stop handing me airplane tickets." He tilted his glass and drank. "Suppose I get the count talking before you arrive?"

"Keep it a secret."

Podret nodded. "The girl—how much does she know?"

"She knows nothing. What she may suspect is something else again."

"That's a good professional answer."

"This is no game for absolutists."

"How right you are." Smoothing the map on the table, he scanned it while Peter opened the wall safe and took out the copies he had made of the two book pages. When Sol looked up Peter said, "There's some interesting genealogy here, Doctor. It might surprise even his daughter."

"But she is not to know?"

"What she doesn't know can't possibly hurt her."

"Another sound professional evasion," Podret rasped. He folded the pages and stuck them in his jacket. "Hell, you're qualified for a Headquarters desk."

"No threats, please. Did you bring sensational new wonder drugs with you? Something sovereign to rend the seven mystic veils?"

"I tucked a few little things in with my drip-dry shirts," he grunted. "You know us behavioral scientists." Then he drained his drink and glanced out of the living room window. "Nice view you've got."

"Yes. And one day I intend to enjoy it."

Podret took a sheet of paper from the back of his wallet and scrutinized it. "Sam Perkins summarized the principal, known events in the count's life: his education and marriage, the battles he fought in during the Civil War, the Blue Division chronology: Grafenwöhr, Grodno, Minsk. And Kowalski gave me the same briefing he gave you—places and prisoner slang."

"You're ready for launching."

"Like a Polaris missile. Well, this has been great, Peter. Two hours after I clear Barajas you boot me out of town in the general direction of Catalonia. Don't think I won't remember your hospitality." Smiling, he went to his room to repack his bag.

Peter drove Dr. Podret as far as Avenida América, pointed out the highway markers, and wished him well. From there Peter taxied back to the Gran Vía and rented a Spanish-made Fiat sedan, one several years old and less conspicuous than the Mercedes.

He followed the Gran Vía to Cibeles Fountain, then took Alcalá as far as Velázquez, and found Hermosilla so choked with chauffeured foreign cars that he parked in a nearby garage and walked back to the Balmoral. This time he sat in a comfortable leather-covered chair at a small table while he sipped *manzanilla* and surveyed the *bon chic* of Madrid. The scent of perfume was as penetrating as that of tobacco smoke, and he noticed a number of middle-aged Continental ladies with manicured young dandies at their sides. Conversely, the older the gentleman, the younger his *amiga* was likely to be, and Peter decided that some tacit code was observed whereby husbands and wives were able to avoid encounters at the Balmoral: odd days of the week, for example, and alternate Saturdays. Whatever the system, it evidently worked.

The ibex racks were still mounted on the walls, and the bustard stared ferociously at the bartenders. The conversational hum stayed at a discreet pitch, and after a while Peter found himself thinking of Beatriz Peralta and her odd-looking escort, and of Don Felipe Carbajal. He wondered whether Beatriz had really planned to deliver the Prados genealogy to Carbajal, or whether Carbajal's name had been invoked on the spur of the moment. If Carbajal had sent her on the mission, what need did he have of the obscure old book? And if Carbajal had not sent her, what was behind Beatriz's evident eagerness? Was the book for herself or for someone else? And did their interest in the book parallel his own?

A face cut across his thoughts; the striking features of a young Andalusian girl leading her aging protector as they neared a corner table. For the Balmoral she was rather extravagantly gowned, with too-red lipstick and dark eye shading, and Peter saw from her covert, darting glances that she realized it. Still, her black hair had been done to perfection, and her smooth skin—the color of wild honey—reminded him abruptly of Paquí.

Paquí, he mused, as the waiter took away his empty glass, and thought that if his business of the night went well, he might go to El Guante before the last show . . . if her troupe was still in Madrid.

Lingering at the Balmoral until the crowd had thinned to a resolute half-dozen, he took a taxi back to Espalter to avoid exposing the Fiat if his apartment were under surveillance. He felt tired and somewhat discouraged as he got into bed, but gradually his preoccupation faded and he slept for two hours.

For dinner he went to the Club 31 on Alcalá, paused at the trout tank, and chose a table next to the wood-paneled wall. The illumination was soft and indirect, and as he read the menu he decided that the succulence of his Gredos catch was still too fresh in his mind to allow him any interest in the restaurant's specimens, so he chose instead *jamón serrano, cocido,* Valencian salad, a delicate goat cheese, and fine, robust coffee. His wine was light Burgos *chorrillo* that passed well over the palate and blended admirably with his food.

Night held the city when he drove his Fiat from the garage, and there was a taste of rain in the air. Moisture diffused the streetlights as he followed the Gran Vía to Plaza España, and when he turned down Calle Ventura Rodríguez he saw pedestrians walking with furled umbrellas.

Peering at street numbers, he drove two blocks before locating the entrance of Beatriz Peralta's apartment house, then went on past it to Ferraz, where he turned around and came back without headlights. He parked on the opposite side of the street no more than fifty yards from the doorway, turned up the collar of his raincoat, and got out his pipe.

Time passed.

The air grew misty, giving the streetlights a blurred, off-focus appearance. People came and went singly and in couples. An occasional car crawled by.

It grew later, and Peter reflected on the remembered luxury of surveillance teams at one's disposal; two men and a transceiver per car. While one man dozed, transceiver action kept the other awake.

On this night a partner would have been more than welcome.

Blinking, he looked away from the entrance to rest his eyes, and when he looked back a figure had materialized near the streetlight. He sat up expectantly, then slumped back as he saw an old woman turn in at the entrance. The kerchief around her hair suggested that she was returning from church.

He lighted his pipe again, stretched his legs in their limited space, and concluded that either he had come too late to see Beatriz depart, or else that she intended staying close to her apartment. But having invested so much time in surveillance, Peter decided on a final try.

Getting quietly out of the car, he walked two blocks to a public telephone, dialed her number, and listened while the telephone rang. After two rings he heard her voice say, "*¿Bueno? ¿Quién habla?*"

"Idiot," he rasped in low, hoarse Spanish, "where have you been? I can't wait all night." Then he hung up and walked back to his car, thinking that where an innocent person would ponder his words and disregard them, someone involved in *konspiratsia* might well react rather than risk being disciplined for having forgotten a rendezvous.

Peter had estimated twenty minutes as maximum reaction time, but after twelve minutes two raincoated figures emerged from the apartment entrance and began to walk toward him.

One was Beatriz, a plastic rain cap drawn over her hair. The man beside her wore a dark felt hat. Even though the man's coat collar was turned up, shielding the lower part of his face, Peter could make out the round shape of his head. The man was something under average height, but still two or three inches taller than Beatriz, and as they passed Peter's car, he saw that they were talking animatedly, the man gesturing with short chops of one hand. Klaus Ehrlich was the name Beatriz had given him.

Peter slid farther down on the seat until his eyes barely reached the window. Then, when they were ten yards beyond him, he sat up and watched them until they disappeared around the corner.

He waited a few moments, then started the engine and backed down the street without turning on his headlights. From the intersection he could see them a block ahead, walking more rapidly now, the man glancing back over his shoulder from time to time.

When they were two blocks distant, he shortened the interval between himself and them by a block, then kept his car idling at the curb. He was on Calle de Ferraz near La Montaña barracks, and the whistle of a train told him that North Station was not far away.

He could barely see the backs of their raincoats when he moved the Fiat forward again, then he saw them blending into the darkness ahead. He put his headlights on, accelerated the Fiat, and caught sight of them at a letter box—a *buzón.*

While the man opened the slot, Beatriz knelt down as though to adjust her shoe. She fumbled in the shadows and stood up. Her hand brushed the side of the box as she turned from it, and then they began walking back toward Peter.

He drove the car past them, head averted, watching the rearview mirror, but neither of them took notice of his car. Estimating their walking time, he idled the Fiat and steered past Calle Ventura Rodríguez just as they turned into the apartment entrance. Then he returned to the *buzón*, glanced around for possible countersurveillance, and began examining the undersurface of the box.

His fingers encountered a jutting block of metal, which slid against the surface as he pressed. Gripping the object, he pulled, and it came free in his palm. Peter walked back to his car, drove around the corner, and braked. Under the dash light his find proved to be a small magnetized metal box, painted on the outside the same color as the letter drop, and with a removable top. Iniside it lay a coil of onionskin paper the diameter of a pencil, on which were printed two words in block letters: *SIN NOVEDAD.*

No news, nothing to report, he translated, recalling the phrase as a laconic password used by Republican armies in the Civil War.

Rewinding the message, he fitted the top back on the cache box, left the car, and replaced the box on the dead drop site—the *dubok*. There was no point in waiting to see who serviced the *dubok,* since Peter himself had provoked the incident. What had been proved was that Beatriz was either a clandestine courier or an active agent, and that much he had already surmised.

Supposing Klaus Ehrlich to be Beatriz's superior—even Volkov himself—the directional flow puzzled him. He had expected Beatriz to attempt to service a drop, not load one, for loading was normally done by an agent at a lower rung on the *apparat* ladder. Then, as he drove away, he theorized that her message was no more than an attempt to remedy the confusion occasioned by his telephone call.

After loading a *dubok*, Soviet agents normally left a signal to indicate the charged condition of the cache—a chalk mark, an open gate, a piece of scrap paper weighted down by a stone—the alternates were varied and infinite, and Peter had thought it wiser to settle for the information already gained rather than spend additional time searching the area to identify the covert indicator.

From his apartment Peter transmitted a message summarizing the night's events, and reporting that Klaus Ehrlich fitted the description of Colonel Sergei Volkov. He did the latter reluctantly and hoped that Headquarters would not send him a swarm of RIS experts whose interests would not necessarily parallel his own. He was too tired to see Paquí, and too many things were on his mind. Some other night he would try again—if he could find time before her troupe left town.

As he got into bed he found himself speculating as to why Ehrlich had accompanied Beatriz to the *dubok*, and wondering what common language they used. Spanish, German, or Russian was the most likely, but if Beatriz spoke Russian the implication was strong that she was no mere *svyazna*—cut-out—but a Soviet-trained illegal agent.

Her alleged fiancé, the late Pablo Martínez Berens, had been a Niño, a repatriated Spanish citizen. Why not Beatriz Peralta as well?

FOURTEEN

That afternoon a Headquarters transmission acknowledged Peter's message and directed him to avoid giving Ehrlich reason to believe that he was under even casual surveillance. A C-3 report dated 1944 indicated that Volkov had served under Berzín in Seville as late as 1938. The message reiterated that no Beatriz Peralta was listed among returnees from the U.S.S.R., and suggested that she was using a false name.

The suggestion added nothing to Peter's store of knowledge, for he had reached the same conclusion; but he was grateful that Headquarters was leaving case control in his hands. As to whether Volkov had been with the Soviet contingent in Spain, C-3 was only an average evaluation, and the report year sourced it to OSS if not MI-6, whose interest in Soviet activities considerably antedated that of the U.S. intelligence community. But if Volkov had spent two years in Spain, the chances were he spoke enough Spanish to make himself understood.

The fundamental question, of course, was whether Ehrlich and Volkov were one and the same—and Headquarters wanted him to stay clear of Ehrlich.

So be it, he thought, picked up the book containing the Prados family tree—all branches of it—and got the Fiat out of the garage. From Espalter he drove north to Calle de Maldonado and parked in front of an old stone-faced residence surrounded by a low iron fence.

He rang the doorbell, waited, then rang again. The door was opened by a stocky man in his late forties whose hair matched the gray whipcord of his chauffeur's uniform. His face was suety, his eyes dull black buttons. The man said curtly, "What do you want?"

"I want to see Señor Carbajal."

"Your business?"

Peter lifted the book. "He wanted this."

"I will give it to him." The man reached for it, but Peter drew the book away.

"I'd prefer to see Señor Carbajal."

"He is—resting this afternoon." The man's eyes moved from Peter's face to the book. "If you want, come back later."

Peter shrugged. "It isn't that important," he said, and handed the book to the man. "Your name?"

"Estanislao," the man rasped. "Yours?"

"Ward. Dr. Ward." Peter smiled winningly. "The book is from the Sainz archives, Estanislao. Remind Señor Carbajal of that when you give it to him."

A grunt was his only response. Peter turned and went down the walk, got into his car, and drove away. After a while he steered down Maldonado again and saw Estanislao in the driveway polishing the headlights of a black Peugeot sedan. Half a block away stood a small panel delivery truck that had been there twenty minutes before, and as Peter passed it he decided that either deliveries in Madrid took excessive time, the truck was out of gas, or it was parked there for a reason.

From Calle de Maldonado he crossed the city and left his car three blocks from the Sainz house, walking the rest of the way. In the library he placed a call to Sol Podret at the Prados *finca* and was told the operator would ring back. To kill time he went into the trophy room, turned on the overhead light, and examined the banners and flags that bore the insignia of regiments and squadrons disbanded more than a quarter of a century before. Pausing at the glass-sided box containing the count's battle beret, he reflected that it was perhaps the only article that could be connected with certainty to the count.

Even lighted the room held a remote, brooding quality. Like a crypt, Peter mused; or a seance where spirits of the restless dead communed with the living.

The telephone rang, and as he walked back toward the library the maid appeared and said the call was for him. Peter expected to hear Sol greeting him, but instead a rough, uncultured voice came over the receiver.

"Estanislao," the caller said. "Don Felipe asked that I thank you for the book and request you to dine with him tonight."

"I'd be happy to. What time?"

"Ten o'clock. Don Felipe recognizes the hour is early, but feels you may want to discuss the future of the Movement with him . . . now that Professor Sainz is no longer among us."

A cute way of putting it, Peter thought. "Ten o'clock," he repeated, and hung up.

Frowning, Peter got up and paced the room. He had planned to leave for the *finca*, but Carbajal's invitation took priority. As yet there was only hearsay connection between the old *impulsor* and Beatriz, but because of Ehrlich's possible identity all her contacts were significant. Peter had planned an appraisal meeting with Carbajal, and the Prados book was to have been the entering wedge. After he had been turned away by Estanislao, Carbajal's surprise invitation exceeded Peter's earlier expectations. He had dangled a nickel's worth of bait and hooked a bar of gold bullion. The return was so disproportionate as to be suspect.

Somewhere in the back of his mind a warning bulb began to flash, sending signals he knew better than to ignore.

Before I bank any gold, he told himself, I'll scratch the surface to verify that it isn't gilt-covered lead.

The telephone rang, and this time Sol Podret's voice came over the wire. "Peter?"

"How'd you know?"

"You're my only friend."

"Right. How are you getting on?"

"Apace is one way of putting it."
"Can you talk?"
"Somewhat."
"Then I'll try questions. Hard case?"
"Plenty."
"Prognosis?"
"Too early, Peter. We've established rapport and that's about all. The girl—Marisa—is mighty helpful, though."
"She's that kind," Peter said. "Have you any plans?"
"Yes, but I'll have to discuss them when you get here. When is that, by the way?"
"I'd planned on being there tonight, but something's come up. You could tell Marisa I'm dining with Carbajal."
Podret grunted. "She won't like that particularly. The old man got the count all upset—something about reviewing his troops. She had a noisy argument with him. Then Coronel Paco arrived this morning, and about all I can say is he's not my type."
"Non-*simpático*, eh? Well, I'll be with you tomorrow, by lunchtime."
"It's quite an establishment, Peter. Horses, cattle, vineyards. Plenty to see and do. When she reached twenty-one, Marisa gave away half the estate to *campesinos*, built homes for them, loaned them money at no interest. I keep asking myself: Can this be Spain?"
"It's enlightened self-interest, Sol. Carry on."
"What else can I do?" Podret said unhappily, and Peter replaced the receiver.
He would have liked to continue following the movements of Beatriz Peralta and her male roommate, but he was under Headquarters instructions to play a distant role. With five hours to kill before he was due at Carbajal's house, Peter telephoned El Guante and extracted the name of Paquí's hotel from the club bookkeeper.
Calling there, he finally reached Paquí and asked her to join him for cocktails, explaining that he was committed for dinner. Rather sulkily she agreed, but when he picked her up in his car he noticed that she wore his new earrings.
They lingered at the Balmoral until the crowd filtered away, then went to a nearby restaurant for a light snack. At nine-thirty Peter took Paquí back to her hotel and promised to meet her at four o'clock. Then he drove to Calle de Maldonado, where he noticed that road-block barriers had been erected to shield workmen who were digging trenches at either end of the block.
As he approached Carbajal's house he saw the black Peugeot in the driveway and wondered if the chauffeur worked nights as well as during the day.

Peter rang the bell, and the door was opened by Estanislao, out of uniform and wearing a blue serge suit. "Come in, Dr. Ward," the chauffeur said.

Taking off his coat, Peter hung it on a rack in the hall and followed Estanislao toward the rear of the house.

"In here," the chauffeur said, halting beside the entrance of a poorly lighted room.

Nodding, Peter stepped inside and paused to peer through the gloom at the two figures that stood facing him in front of the fireplace. He had been expecting to find only Carbajal in the room, not the man and woman who stared at him with fixed smiles on their faces. Peter glanced quickly to left and right, his eyes searching the room for Carbajal, but the old man was not there—not in the room. Instead, he was facing Beatriz and Ehrlich. His stomach froze and his muscles stiffened.

No one spoke.

Stepping back, Peter started to turn, remembered Estanislao, and moved more quickly.

But he had remembered too late, and as he ducked he heard the sound of expelled air, the swish of an object moving rapidly through space, and then the back of his head exploded in a sheet of pain. Crumpling, he felt another blow less painful than the first as he drowned in a gulf of darkness.

Minutes or hours later his first sensation was of pain; pain related to motion. He was in a hammock that swayed, each movement thrusting blood through battered veins. Not a hammock; he was held by feet and shoulders. He was being carried. Voices penetrated his brain, short, guttural words; a man was giving orders in a foreign tongue: "*Atroyti dver.*" Night air touched his face, cool, healing air, then his body was jerked roughly and swung against something hard. He tried to move his arms, but his hands were bound behind him. He wanted to open his eyes, but he kept them shut. The hands left his body, and he realized that he was lying on the floor in the back of a car. Voices again, speaking Russian:

"*Kotoriy chas?*"

"*Dvinatsot chisof.*"

"*Kto on takoy?*"

"*Miy znayim shto on Amerikanits.*"

A woman's voice. "*Nuzhno eto?*" Beatriz.

"*Eto ochin nuzhno.*"

"*Kak mne nuzhno iti?*" Estanislao.

"*Idity pramo. Ponimayiti?*"

"*Ya nichivo ni ponimayo.*" Estanislao again.

Light stabbed his eyelids—a flashlight beam, he reasoned, and lay limp until it disappeared.

"*Idity skareyo! Do svidaniyo.*"

Do svidaniyo, Peter echoed silently. Good-bye.

The car engine started, making the floor vibrate under his back. Pain ballooned through his body; the taste of bile rose in his throat.

The car moved slowly ahead; cautiously, stealthily. As far as his stunned brain could grasp, it was heading for the street. Gritting his teeth, he forced his back up against the door, shoving his bound feet, until his eyes were level with the window. The car slanted forward as it left the driveway and turned to the right.

Ahead stood the construction barriers, the white wood striped with black paint visible in the lanterns' glow. The barriers were offset so that two sharp turns were required to pass through them. A gear shifted, and the car gathered speed.

Peter closed his eyes as a jolt shot fresh pain through his throbbing head.

The car accelerated, and Peter opened his eyes again, wondering when the driver would slow. Suddenly the interior of the car was flooded with blinding light. The driver gave a guttural cry and shaded his eyes with a hand.

From the barrier came a warning shout.

Then things happened so rapidly that Peter's dulled reflexes had no time to react. The car lurched ahead, wood smashed across the nose of the car, and shots rang out. The car slammed across an obstacle and pitched downward to a crashing halt, slamming Peter's body against the back of the front seat. In a blur of motion the driver wrenched open his door and burst out. Voices shouted commands, but the man kept moving. He rose from the shallow trench that held the car and began running forward. Turning, he fired his pistol at the blinding lights. Then a burst of fire caught him, jerking his body around, his hands flailing the empty air. His legs thrust him forward, but awkwardly, like a one-winged moth beating its circle of death. Then his body toppled to one side, and as Peter struggled to lift his head into the zone of light men raced toward the fallen body. A siren wailed, and from the far end of the street a police car shot into view.

As men gathered around the dead man Peter shouted. He shouted again until a man left the group and raced toward him, jumped into the trench, and pried open the jammed rear door.

"*¡Diablo!*" the man shouted, and beckoned to his comrades. Then his hands began untying the cord around Peter's wrists.

When his hands were free Peter pointed at his feet and felt himself being drawn out of the door. They leaned him against the fresh-dug earth to untie his feet, then helped him upright, steadying him while he gulped great breaths of air.

One of the spotlights died out, but light from another showed Fermín Hernández walking toward the holed-in car, and it dawned on Peter that this was a police operation. A trap had been set and closed.

He stared beyond Hernández at the dead face of Estanislao as men lifted the body onto a stretcher. Peter touched the back of his head and felt his stomach turn over. Weakly he moved toward the detective, who blurted, "Dr. Ward!"

"What's left of me." Swallowing, he wet dry lips.

"Costa was going to kill you, too?" he demanded.

"Costa?" Peter said huskily.

"Estanislao Costa." He gestured over his shoulder at the stretcher. "He killed one Pablo Martínez. Why did he want to kill you?"

"Ask Carbajal."

Hernández shook his head. "Don Felipe has a fine public reputation. What has he to do with all this?"

"He asked me to dine tonight. When I arrived Costa struck me down."

"You are a man marked for violence," Hernández said cryptically. "First a bomb, then—" He shrugged. "Was Carbajal present?"

"He must have been."

The detective's eyes narrowed. "You saw him? Think—this is a grave charge."

"No," Peter said. "I did not see him."

"Who did you see?"

"Estanislao," Peter said slowly. He closed his eyes and steadied himself against a rail of the smashed barrier. "A woman named Peralta—Beatriz Peralta. She worked for Professor Sainz and lived on Ventura Rodríguez." Opening his eyes, he took a deep breath. "They may still be in the house."

"They?"

"A man was with her—Klaus Ehrlich is his name."

Turning, Hernández ordered three men to search Carbajal's house, and as they jogged away, Peter walked unsteadily to the curb and sat down. The stretcher was inside the panel truck now. The police car moved away to let it leave. Looking down at Peter, the detective said, "What do you know of this business?"

"I'm working in the Royalist archives. Beatriz Peralta worked there while Sainz was alive, and I met Carbajal at his funeral. Today I took a book to him and he asked me to dine with him. When I arrived—"

"What time?" the detective broke in.

"Ten."

Hernández looked at his watch. "It is nearly twelve now. Go on."

Nearly two hours unconscious, Peter thought, licked his lips again, and tried not to think of his pulsing head. "Estanislao took me back to the sitting room. Carbajal was not there. I saw Beatriz and this man Ehrlich, and then Estanislao struck me down from behind."

"That is how he killed Pablo Martínez," the detective remarked. "A pipe was recovered from the area of the wreckage. It had the blood and hair of Martínez and the fingerprints of Costa." Taking out a notebook, he wrote on it briefly. "We will get to the bottom of this, my friend," he said, "but you will find that Don Felipe Carbajal is guilty of nothing more than hiring Estanislao Costa."

Peter was about to protest when he saw one of the policemen walking back from Carbajal's house. The policeman said to Hernández, "There was no one inside the house."

"You see?" Hernández said. "Like yourself, Felipe Carbajal has been victimized."

"*Que lástima,*" Peter said bitterly. "Are you going to question him?"

"Most assuredly, *señor*. Just as soon as he returns to Madrid."

"From where?" Peter snapped.

Hernández shrugged. "From Cataluña—from the Prados *finca*."

Peter's eyes narrowed. "How do you know he is there?"

Wearily, Hernández shook his head. "Señor—today you called a person at the Prados *finca*, no?"

"*Sí.*"

"That person mentioned to the *condesa* that you were dining with Don Felipe, eh?"

"Go on."

"And the *condesa*, knowing Don Felipe could not be in Madrid when he was in Cataluña, requested us to investigate the affair. Is it now clear?"

"Transparently."

"Now, of course," Hernández went on, "we might have been less interested had we not already determined Costa's address. That fact, plus the *condesa's* request, accounts for this"—his hand gestured at the barriered trenches, the wrecked car—"this scene of destruction."

"Excellent," Peter rasped. "What about Beatriz Peralta?"

"She will be questioned, have no fear. But without witnesses it will be difficult to implicate her in this outrage. As a lawyer you should appreciate the situation."

"All too well," Peter said. He stood up and winced with pain.

As he began walking away, Hernández called, "We will drive you wherever you care to go."

"Never mind," Peter said. "I have a car."

Reaching the Fiat, he got inside, put his hands on the wheel, and saw that they were trembling. His headlights caught the black Peugeot sedan tilting down into the trench, barrier wood splintered crazily about it. The last floodlight went out, and men began rigging a new barrier across Calle de Maldonado. They hung lighted lanterns on it to protect other cars from the trench, picked up their tools, and left.

He had a message to transmit to Langley, he told himself. And after that—if two or three hours' sleep improved the way he felt—a four-o'clock date with Paquí.

Slowly his vision cleared, and when his hands were steady he started the engine and drove away.

Part IV

Dawn had become a friend. Dawn washed the sky with broad, changing paths of pink and lavender, and the brown earth seemed to cling to the slowly rising sun. With it came a cool breeze bearing the scent of thyme, then warming wind swirling little whorls of dust upward until they thinned and vanished. Birds sang, and from distant pastures came the stirring of wakened cattle, the chime of ox bells, the plodding of horses' hooves.

Branches moved in the breeze, and the sun made silver coins of their oval leaves. The well pulley creaked, and in the kitchen the cook began a lilting song in Catalan.

It was enough, he thought, to lie quietly in his bedroom and hear and see through the window the pleasures of early morning. He had come back to Cataluña after half a lifetime away, and here he had found friends, new friends—better friends than those he had known in his youth.

Sol was sun, warm and cheerful; a good friend to walk with and talk to. A fine, honest man who listened and encouraged him and told him that one day he would be able to remember everything he cared to remember—even to the daughter he had never known before.

Riding the rocky hills, they spoke of battles and the Movement and death of many men, the Passion of Spain that had been before the tortures and the endless snows, hunger, death, and dying of Vorkuta. When he spoke of the con-

demned—kontriki—*Sol understood; he understood the bribery system*—tufta—*and how they killed* suki—*informers—whenever they could manage to without reprisal.*

These were the things he could never bring himself to talk of with Marisa lest she shrink from the defilement he had lived. But with Sol it was different; a man understood and could in friendship be trusted with many things.

It seemed that Sol was one of Marisa's friends, a Spanish-speaking foreigner; small and gentle and wise. It was he who suggested—when they walked in the woods one day—the building of an isba, *a copy of the miserable log hut he had lived in his last two years as a free worker. So the two of them had begun to fell dead trees with their axes and build it in a secret place. Sol promised him that sometime after it was finished he would bring Marisa to see it and explain what it was and how her father had built the first one alone from logs whose sap was as hard as frozen amber.*

Through the open window drifted the fragrance of frying bread and meat, coffee and boiling milk. His mouth watered and he sat up, then left the bed and turned on the hot shower, letting the bathroom fill with steam. When he had scrubbed himself he began to seek lice, remembered that he was free of them, and lifted his gaze to stare in the mirror at his body. His ribs were knotted with old healed breaks, his chest, arms, and legs covered with scars, some still faintly blue: the marks of burns, bayonets, and bullets, the whiplash of a broken cable, the stabs of blatnyaki *knives.*

After so many years of seeing himself infrequently in a piece of broken mirror—and finding a bearded, rag-covered prisoner—he was unaccustomed to looking at himself full length and naked. Of some scars he had no recollection, no means of determining their cause—the deep pit on his right hip, the scar that followed the angle of his right cheekbone. He fingered it uncertainly, trying to gain even a faint memory of its cause; then his hand began to tremble, and he turned from the mirror to dry himself and reach the kitchen before all the food was gone.

After he had eaten, he told himself, he would take his axe and go to the woods and begin work even before his friend was awake.

FIFTEEN

It was a piece of good luck, Peter reflected, that Estanislao Costa's choice of weapon had been a cosh rather than the cyanide pistol of Bogdan Stashinsky, Khoklov, and other assassins of the Ninth Section. But it was bad luck that the police had shot him down.

Alive, Costa might have given information regarding the GRU net to which he belonged, enough perhaps to identify the *rezident*. Dead, he was just another sacrifice to the Soviet *konspiratsia*, and would quickly be forgotten.

Peter sat in a comfortable chair on the shaded porch of the Prados *finca* house and watched cloud shadows move across the purple foothills. The drive from Madrid had tired him, and he was glad of a chance to relax before Marisa, the count, and Sol Podret returned.

By now Klaus Ehrlich and Beatriz would be underground with new names and identity papers, sheltered in some emergency *yafka*—unless they had already left Spain. At least a part of their objective had been accomplished, he felt; Sainz had been disposed of and the man who had liquidated his killer was dead, and none of the crimes was traceable to the U.S.S.R. Carbajal remained, of course, but as far as the Madrid police were concerned, he was clean.

With a grunt of disgust Peter felt for his pipe and got it going. His head still pained and his shoulder ached from the impact of the Peugeot against the ditch, but he was disinclined to baby himself; things could have been a hell of a lot worse.

As he smoked in the quiet solitude of the warm afternoon he found himself nodding, and when his pipe died out he laid it aside and dozed in the cushioned chair.

Hoofbeats woke him, and he opened his eyes to see Marisa cantering toward him on a palomino. She wore the round, flat-brimmed *sombrero andaluz* held in place by a chin strap, and as she posted, a long plait of hair flicked over the shoulder of her white, ruffle-front hacking shirt. Peter waved and stood up and she waved back, leaving her mount as it slowed, and running toward him.

Black suede trousers covered the tops of her dusty riding boots, and as she took the low porch steps in a stride she tossed her riding crop into a chair, then met his arms.

Peter gave her an avuncular kiss, stepped back, and looked at her tanned face and wide, clear eyes.

"Oh, Peter, I've missed you! It's *so* good to have you here."

"I've missed you," he said, and realized as he spoke that he had missed her more than he ought to say. "Where's Sol and the count?"

"In the woods." She let the hat slide behind her head and opened her shirt collar. Turning toward the screen door, she called, "*María. Sangría para nosotros, por favor.*"

"*Sí, condesa, en seguida,*" came the reply, as Marisa blotted her face with a handkerchief and settled into a chair.

"How long have you been here?"

"An hour," he said, "maybe a little longer."

"I'm sorry I wasn't here to greet you. The servants showed you to your room?"

"In fine style." Resuming his chair, he filled his pipe and lighted it. "What are they doing in the woods? Bird-watching?"

She shook her head. "Dr. Podret—I mean Sol—says it's a form of therapy for my father. They're building a log hut together, but I'm not supposed to know about it. Father wants me to learn only gradually about the horrible life he lived."

"That's understandable, but why the log hut?"

"It's a replica of the hovel my father lived in after he was released from Vorkuta—when he worked outside the prison compound." Sitting forward, she said, "I can't tell you how grateful I am to you for bringing Sol here. In just these few days Father's come to regard him as a friend, someone he can trust and confide in. Sol's a fine person, isn't he?"

"One of the best," Peter agreed, as a plump maid came out of the house bearing a silver tray with a sweating silver pitcher.

Marisa filled two glasses with claret-colored *sangría*, and Peter drank the wine-juice mixture thirstily. He refilled their glasses and saw that she was gazing toward the foothills, a remote expression in her eyes. "What happened last night?"

"At Carbajal's house? The police had the place under surveillance. Estanislao tried to run and ended up in the ditch. Dead."

"And you?"

"I was lucky—thanks to your foresight." He cleared his throat. "Pablo Martínez killed Don Eduardo, Estanislao killed Pablo, and the police killed him."

Her forehead furrowed. "You're displeased?"

He shrugged. "Estanislao didn't hatch the plot, Marisa; whoever directed him is still at large."

"Ready to place another bomb under your bed."

"Who told you?" he said sharply.

"Even in the police we have friends, members of the Movement. Someone informed Paco, and Paco told me. In this country a secret is as perishable as a snowflake."

"I'll remember that. Don Felipe quarreled with you, Marisa. Over what?"

"The same thing: whether and when my father should appear before the Brigadas." Then her lips trembled. "Oh, Peter, I'm so afraid of doing wrong. I'm not a political person—I shouldn't have to decide what course the Movement will take."

"You inherited responsibility."

"Responsibility," she said bitterly. "A male word, part of the *machismo* that burdens Spain. We women must be so perfect, so chaste—while our men . . ." Her mouth turned down scornfully.

"Then let Sol decide when your father should appear before the Brigadas."

Her face relaxed and suddenly she smiled. "Of course! I should have thought of that—but then," she went on with a certain coquetry, "I don't have a mind like yours—a man's mind."

"You have a remarkable mind," he said, and relighted his pipe. Marisa drew off her hard felt hat and began undoing her braid. Shaking her hair free, she separated the tresses with her fingers and arranged them over her shoulders. She looked now, he thought, no more than eighteen, and unbelievably lovely. Sipping from her glass, she said, "You like Spain, do you not?"

"Of course."

"Would you—have you ever thought of living here—in Spain, I mean?" she finished awkwardly, and he thought he detected sudden color in her tanned cheeks.

Deliberately he said, "Everyone's dreamed of castles in Spain, Marisa. It's a byword for paradise." Then he gathered some lumps of sugar from the tray, rose, and walked to where the palomino was resting.

Stroking the gelding's muzzle and mane, Peter fed it sugar a lump at a time and heard Marisa's boots treading the earth behind him. She picked up the trailing reins and laid them across the cushioned pommel.

In a taut voice she said, "Peter—I don't mean just anyone's vague notions of Old Castile—I mean do you think *you* could be happy here—in a place like this? For the rest of your life?"

His throat had gone dry. He tried to look away, but her eyes held him. "I—" he began, and swallowed. "I suppose it would depend."

"Then suppose," she said throatily, and laid one hand on his, "suppose you were to live here with me."

With difficulty he took a deep breath. There was this girl . . . and there was his mission. His work and—Marisa. "Every man searches for a woman like you," he said huskily. "The hard part is finding her."

He kissed her temple wordlessly. Then, hand in hand, they went into the big house.

When the sun touched the mountains they rode together through olive groves and down to a cool fresh stream, Peter on a chestnut stallion whose easy gait reminded him of his own coal-black hunter. And as they rode back in the twilight they saw two distant men walking slowly through the fields toward the house.

Sol Podret came into Peter's room, said, "Believe me, I'm glad to see you!" and held out blistered, callused hands. His face and arms were sunburned, and the top of his head was peeling.

"You look fit," Peter told him.

"And I've lost three kilos." Sol pounded his midriff. "Actually," he said as he lay down on the bed, "I've never felt better in my life. My God, when I left Washington I never thought I'd end up chopping trees in Catalonia! And the count's a rugged specimen, for all he's gone through. What a worker!" Groaning, he sat up and fished a cigarette from a limp package. "I suppose you want a report? Well, rapport's established—the transfer's taken place, though I'm not sure from what."

Peter grinned. "You make a wonderful father figure."

"So my wife tells me. I've cast you in a different role, though. You'll be the hard voice of implacable authority."

"The bad cop and the good cop," Peter said reflectively. "Say on, dear and glorious physician."

Podret grimaced. "We're building an *isba*—thank God it's almost finished—and after that I've got another project."

"Build thee more stately mansions—" Peter quoted almost inaudibly, breaking off at Sol's frown. "Sorry—I'm a little distracted."

"You? Distracted?"

Peter nodded. "I've just skinned through what sounded very much like a proposal of marriage."

Podret gaped at him. "*Marisa?*"

"María Luisa Pérez y Vals Delgado, Condesa de Prados."

"How lucky can you get!" Rumpling his hair, Podret shook his head. "Beauty, wealth, and position. How soon do you post the banns?"

"I've temporized. Now what is your next construction project?"

The psychiatrist sighed. "As usual, Peter, we operate on two separate levels. Me in the kitchen with the pot-wallopers while you whirl the princess around the floor." He cleared his throat. "A *sobatschnik.*"

"Why?"

"To explore his subconscious more profoundly." Podret got up and began pacing the floor. "If I can simulate one of the worst experiences in Rodrigo's life, get him to relive it, maybe I can break through his memory block."

"Is that sound therapy?"

"It's done every day. Narcosynthesis."

Peter grimaced.

"You've got scruples?"

"Not if it's the only way."

"All right. It's the only way *I* know to do the job in a reasonable period of time. Time *is* a factor, isn't it?"

"More than ever," Peter said, and told him about Beatriz, Estanislao, and Ehrlich. When he had finished, Sol switched on a floor lamp, drew it beside Peter, and examined his eyes carefully.

"A little bloodshot," he muttered, then peered at the scabbed bruise on the back of Peter's head. "Nothing broken, I guess, but you were plenty lucky." He turned off the lamp. "I'll set it up, then—the *sobatschnik,* I mean. You'll tell Marisa?"

Peter tugged the lobe of one ear.

"Are you going to tell Marisa?"

"I'm not sure."

Podret grunted. "We need a house, Peter—a basement to work in. If Marisa isn't cut in we're making it unnecessarily difficult."

"What if the man she accepts as her father turns out to be an impostor?"

The psychiatrist shrugged. "It's our job to find out—at least I thought it was."

"Whatever the outcome, it's privileged information. Try the hard way first, and if the obstacles are insuperable I'll look for another way."

After Sol went to his own room, Peter lay back on his bed and turned his head so that he could look out into the purpling dusk. Last night, he remembered, only the voice of Beatriz Peralta had questioned what the others were planning to do with him. *Is this necessary*? she had asked, and Ehrlich's bland retort had been, *This is very necessary.* At least she had a few vestiges of human feeling, he reflected, and murmured *Spasibo, Tovarich Beatriz. Spasibo.*

His thoughts turned to Marisa and her halting, half-shy words, their unmistakable intent. Puppy love, he told himself uncomfortably, the infatuation of a sheltered child. But as he thought of her he remembered his own long loneliness, and he became less sure that what she felt for him was fugitive and immature.

Every man has a Granada locked in a secret corner of his mind, he mused. Perhaps mine is here in Catalonia—this place between Lérida and Borjas. Then, against that enticing prospect, he stacked the years spent in secret intelligence with their frustrations and defeats, their risks and hazards, and considered the years of silent combat ahead. And he found himself wondering whether now was not the time to leave, quit, get out with a whole skin, and lead a simple, open life, with a wife again, and with children.

Drowsily his eyes closed; he felt ineffably peaceful and secure.

When Sol Podret stopped by before dinner, he found Peter asleep.

SIXTEEN

Sol and the count constructed the *sobatschnik* in the murky heat of an empty stone silo half a mile from the main house. Peter was responsible for decoying Marisa from the site, which he did through the device of long picnic rides to the far reaches of the *finca*, with the unwitting assistance of Paco Arastegui, who was only too glad to accompany Marisa as Peter's occasional alternate.

The next step was to isolate the count long enough to carry through the balance of their plan, and an opportunity came in the form of a High Mass held at the old Lérida cathedral to memorialize the Royalist dead of the Civil War.

Podret persuaded Marisa to leave the count in his charge while Paco took her to Lérida, where they were to be joined by Felipe Carbajal and others of the Royalist hierarchy.

They drove away in the early morning with some of the *finca* servants, and when they were gone, Podret took two small, brownish-colored tablets from his shaving kit and dropped them into the pocket of his coat.

"I'll breakfast with Rodrigo," he told Peter, "and slip them in his coffee."

"Powerful stuff?"

"It'll wax your car, fill your cavities, and run off with your mother-in-law."

"Very funny. What is it?"

"An improvement over LSD 25, with reserpine. Basically, it's a hallucinogen that allows certain perceptual reactions." He took a deep breath. "The moment of truth, Peter—in every sense."

From his bedroom window Peter watched Sol and the count leave the house and walk off in the direction of the silo. He was to follow in thirty minutes, ample time to eat breakfast, but he was too tense for food, and his stomach knotted as he reviewed his role in the psychodrama the three of them were to enact.

His pipe tasted old and flat so he put it away, looked at his watch again, and drove the Fiat over the rutted trail that led to the silo. When he reached it, he saw Sol open the wooden door and step quickly outside.

Leaving the car, Peter walked toward him and saw Podret wet his lips. The psychiatrist said huskily, "He's reacting well, Peter; I've taken him back to his boyhood. You've never done this before, and I'll tell you it's eerie. You're the interrogator, remember—one of those MVD sons of bitches. Live the part."

Peter grimaced, said, "Let's go," and stooped to pass under the doorway's wood lintel.

The silo had been built of fieldstone with a wooden roof, and the interior stank of sour silage and earth. Even now, with the sun risen only a few hours, the heat was stifling.

What light there was came from a screened lantern on the earth floor a dozen feet behind the *sobatschnik*.

They had built the kennel of old lumber, a meter high, a meter long, and two feet wide. There were chinks between some of the weathered boards, and a cluster of air holes were drilled in the top. To Peter, in the flickering light, it looked like a crude packing case, but he knew that inside it, animal-like, crouched a nearly naked man, sweating and gasping hot, fetid air.

Atop the *sobatschnik* sat a recorder small enough to fit inside a hollowed-out medical book, and Peter saw the soft glint of the round metal microphone, the slowly turning reels.

Pulling off his shirt, he licked dry lips and moved to the side of the *sobatschnik* as Podret took up his position on the other side. The odor of the close air was sickening. Somewhere in the crepuscular gloom, beyond the reach of the lantern, an animal made a rustling sound, and now Peter could hear the count's labored breathing.

Only geography separated the scene from a cell in Lefortovo or the Lubianka, he thought, and steeled himself to say in curt Russian: "Citizen, you are accused of grave crimes against the Soviet state. Citizen, you will state your name."

There was a moment of utter silence, and then from the wooden kennel came a man's drugged voice. "My name, Comrade Citizen, is Feodor Voskrisenye."

"You dare call me Comrade?" Peter snarled. "Think well of your position, Citizen Voskrisenye!"

"I—I was wrong, Citizen Examiner," came the humble reply. "I will not again degrade you."

It works, Peter thought in awe. It really *works*. Then, with a glance at Podret's intent face, he said accusingly, "Your name was not always Feodor Voskrisenye."

"True, Citizen Examiner. The name is one I adopted for convenience in the Soviet Union."

"Your name at birth?"

"Ramón," said the detached, hollow voice. "Ramón Baeza."

Peter raised his eyes and looked at Podret, who held up a warning hand. If what the crouching man had said was true—and in the bowels of the Lubianka, prisoners spoke only truth—it ran counter to all the known facts of the count's birth. For the count's family name was Pérez, his matronymic Vals Salvat, and his Christian names Jaime and Rodrigo.

Peter dragged air into his lungs and rasped, "How is this, Citizen? Perhaps we had better go back a little. Where were you born?"

"In Spain, Citizen Examiner," the voice said respectfully.

Yes, the Conde de Prados had been born in Spain. "Province?"

"Gerona, Citizen Examiner—a province of Cataluña."

Correct. But something was out of key. He saw Podret bend close to the air holes and say in a soft voice. "My friend, it is better to tell the truth. For the sake of both of us, have confidence in Soviet justice. Only the truth, Comrade, and I promise you this will pass."

A sense of loathing came over Peter. Here in the vault-like dimness it would be all too easy to forget reality and become, in fact, the citizen examiner. He shook himself and went on. "Your dossier states you fought in the Spanish uprising."

"Indeed, Citizen Examiner, that is true. I was a loyal soldier in that terrible war."

"Name the battles in which you took part."

The man's breathing harshened, and Podret uncovered more air holes. Peter wiped sweat from his face and wondered how long they could go on—any of them. After a few moments he repeated the question, and the prisoner replied dully, "Belchite—the four days of Belchite."

Right. The blue *boina* with its engraved legend was lasting evidence of that battle.

"Lérida," the prisoner rasped in an anguished voice. "Lérida—so near my home."

Peter saw the psychiatrist nod. This was like catechizing a child.

"Albacete."

Peter's eyes narrowed. He had not known the count was at Albacete.

"Manzanares."

Unknown.

"Andujar."

Again unknown. Two positives and three doubtful.

Peter cleared his throat. "What of Granada, Citizen Prisoner? What of Talavera de la Reina and the Coruña Road?"

Silence was his only response. Finally the count gasped. "It is wrong, Citizen Examiner. In the battles I fought I bore myself bravely, but I never fought in those battles." His voice became covert, doubtful. "I—have I been denounced for cowardice?"

Peter looked blankly at Sol Podret, who shook his head, then bent over the air holes. "It is true, Comrade Voskrisenye, that you have been denounced, but not for cowardice. Think, my friend—did you play no part at Granada? At the battle of Coruña Road?"

"I—I swear it," came the hoarse reply. "I swear it is the truth—on the grave of my mother."

Podret looked up at Peter, then said gently, "The citizen examiner will give you a period in which to recall, Comrade Feodor. He is patient and will return to you again. For the present you must sleep. Rest until I waken you."

Rising, he gestured at the doorway, and walked toward it, followed by Peter.

Outside, they gulped great lungsful of air, wiped their torsos dry, and moved to the shady side of the stone tower.

When his breathing slowed, Podret said, "I don't get it, Peter. He says he wasn't in those three battles, and he wasn't lying." He wiped his forehead again. "He *can't* lie—the inhibitors aren't functioning."

Peter looked away from his colleague, at the pastures and woods, the ragged mountains beyond. He was shaken by the experience; the raw brutality of the reenactment, the unreal, seancelike quality.

"You don't like it," Podret said after a while.

"I hate it."

Sol laid an arm over his shoulder. "I hate it, too," he said gently, "dissecting a man's brain cell by cell. But we've only begun, Peter. Let's get it over with."

Peter sucked in a hissing breath. "I'm no good at this, Sol. I'd rather be in the kennel than doing what I'm doing."

"Buck up, lad. He's not really conscious of any of this. It's a dream he's living through, and it's harmless."

"He's suffering, Goddamn it! Will he remember?"

"Only what I allow him to remember." He shook his head. "Peter, this sort of thing is my life—my profession. Trust me."

Turning, Peter began walking toward the closed door, then halted. "Why did he choose Voskrisenye as a name? The only other man who ever called himself Sunday was named Billy. Even in Russian it's rare."

"Sunday," Sol said thoughtfully. "*Domingo* in Spanish. There's your answer."

"The count wasn't named Domingo—you know that." Almost savagely he opened the door and strode to the wooden cell.

When Podret was in position again he said, "Wake, now, Comrade Feodor. The citizen examiner is here."

Then for a quarter of an hour Peter led the count back over the battlefields of a quarter of a century before, but when he realized that he could not change the prisoner's story he returned to the count's boyhood and his family.

"You were born in Gerona province," he challenged. "In what city?"

"No city, Citizen Examiner," the prisoner said wearily, "but a small town. I was born on a farm near Borjas."

The Prados estate was near Borjas, but the *finca* could never conceivably be referred to as a farm. Peter glanced significantly at Podret. "The dossier classifies your parents as aristocrats. What do you say to that?"

"It is true, Citizen Examiner. My late father was an aristocrat."

"And your mother? Doña Emilia?"

"Doña Emilia?" the troubled voice mused. "My mother was Doña Manuela Baeza. A fine woman, Citizen Examiner, and of the working class."

Peter stared at the air holes through which the voice filtered. He said quickly, "Your father was the Conde de Prados?"

"Yes, Citizen Examiner." The man coughed hoarsely. "Don

Domingo Pérez. My mother was—she was not his wife."

Podret rose from his crouch, and Peter nodded gratefully. Wiping his face, he glanced upward at cracks of light gleaming between the roof boards. The sun angle had reached somewhere between 30 and 40 degrees. His head pounded from the foul, heated air.

Sitting down, he held his head with his hands and visualized again the final page in the book that held the Prados genealogy. Beside the names of Don Domingo and Doña Emilia, Eduardo Sainz had penciled another name: *Manuela Baeza,* and had drawn intersecting lines from her name and that of Don Domingo. At the point of intersection he had printed the name *Ramón,* and written very faintly after it, *ilegítimo.*

The man in the *sobatschnik* was not Jaime Rodrigo Pérez but a half-brother, unacknowledged and unknown to all but a very few. He was not Marisa's father but her uncle.

Peter looked up at Podret and saw him gesturing at his watch. They were running short of time.

He got to his feet again and breathed the fetid air. Half the mystery was solved, but more remained. How had Ramón gotten to Russia? When had he gone? And why had he come back? Setting his teeth, Peter said, "Very well, Citizen Prisoner. We make no distinction between marriage and nonmarriage, and your lack of a bourgeois background inclines me to view you in a favorable light."

"Oh, thank you, Citizen Examiner—"

"You may refer to me as Comrade."

Peter wiped his lips and ignored the question on Podret's face. Tapping his wristwatch, he moved ahead. "Your half-brother, Count Rodrigo, fought with the Nationalists. On which side were you?"

"The side of the Republic," came the reply. "I was a fighter for socialism."

"I understand. Now—how did you manage to reach the Soviet Union?"

"By sea, Comrade Examiner. We came—many of us across the Pyrenees and into France. A ship of the Soviet Union brought me to Odessa. It was the *Piatiletka.*"

Peter cleared his throat. The temperature, he thought, must be well over 100 degrees. "Comrade Feodor, how did your difficulties with the Soviet authorities begin?"

The man in the kennel paused. "Comrade Examiner—if you will permit me—my difficulties are with those Spaniards who suddenly became our leaders here in the Soviet Union. Along with many others I protested the informal transfer of Republican gold to the Soviet authorities."

"Do you know how much gold was involved?"

Ramón Baeza said hesitantly, "Señor Negrín told us it was worth two and a half billion pesetas."

Accurate, Peter thought. Details of the Spanish gold shipment had been vetted for a quarter of a century and were now well known. Dying in Mexico, Negrín had willed the documents to Franco.

Podret whispered something to the prisoner, who said, "Yes. I was released from Novostroika to fight with partisans in the Ukraine. Then, after victory, I was arrested again, charged with having had suspicious contact with the German enemy, and sent to Vorkuta. When my time was up I was released. Because I had no family in the Soviet Union I stayed as a free worker."

"Your scar—" Peter began, but stopped at a wave of Podret's hand.

The psychiatrist said, "Comrade Feodor, if you have no family in the Soviet Union, where is your family?"

The drugged man said almost slyly, "The Soviet authorities know."

"I am your friend," Podret said calmly. "You may tell me."

In a hoarse whisper Ramón said, "After I was arrested my wife and child were deported to the Estonian Autonomous Republic. Her Spanish name is Juana, but in Russian she is known as Vera. My daughter is named Sonia."

Dragging the back of his hand across his dripping neck, Peter said, "Your scar, Comrade Feodor. Was it gained in battle?"

Again the answering voice was cautious. "No, Comrade Examiner."

Then Podret said, "Feodor, confide in me."

"The scar—" the voice said faintly. "No . . ."

"Continue," Podret said firmly. "You acquired the scar in Vorkuta?"

"It . . ." the voice said dully. "It began when I was called to the Central Camp Administration hut. An officer of the MVD from Moscow talked to me—he was the first officer of the MVD who treated me other than as a beast." His voice rose unevenly. "They would release me, he said. They would send me back to Spain in three or four years if I would cooperate—carry out his orders." His voice broke off, and Peter could hear the gasp of indrawn breath.

"Slowly, Comrade Feodor," Podret counseled. "Have no fear."

On the recorder box a red light glowed, a warning that the tape was almost unwound. Peter stared at it and heard Ramón's faint voice again. "In the camp hospital I was operated on—they did not tell me why. But when I woke there was this—bandage, and as long as I was in the hospital I was allowed two men's rations. The food was good, and it was warm." A note of remembered pleasure crept into his voice. "So warm . . . and afterward I was given lighter duties. . . ."

His voice trailed off, and they heard his body slump forward in the crate.

At once Podret threw open the top and Peter pushed out the silo door. Cool air flooded in, and Peter gulped it like an exhausted swimmer. Podret came toward him unsteadily. "Finished, Peter?"

"No."

A muscle twitched in Podret's face. "He can't take much more."

"I need the name of his contact in Spain. I want details of the plan, the bargain the Soviets made."

Podret blotted his face. "The last seems clear enough: Ramón is here. His wife and child are hostages."

When Peter said nothing, the psychiatrist said, "Let me ask him, Peter. Then the responsibility is mine."

Nodding, Peter stopped the tape recorder and reversed the reel. From the distance came a hum like a low-flying plane.

Together they pulled Ramón from the *sobatschnik* and laid him on the packed-earth floor. Unseen animals rustled through shreds of silage. The lantern guttered out.

Kneeling beside the unconscious man, Podret began to speak to him, and after a while his eyes opened. Slowly, haltingly, he answered the psychiatrist's questions. Through the camp underground he had learned that his wife and child had died in an epidemic, but the Soviet authorities did not know that he knew; if he had told them he would not have been allowed to go to Spain. A man named Carbajal had given him his instructions: Incite the Royalists against the government.

"How—" Peter began, but Podret shook his head, reached for the water bottle, and helped the prone man to drink. Then he got up and shut off the recorder. "He needs rest, Peter."

"How soon can we move him?"

"Not for ten minutes. I want his respiration and temperature to normalize."

The low-flying aircraft was coming nearer. It seemed almost overhead when Peter heard a bump, the jarring of a vehicle, and the skid of tires on the dirt road. Tensing, he glanced warningly at Podret, and was striding toward the doorway when a figure blocked it.

"*Dios*!" came the hoarse voice of Paco. "What have you

done to him?" And as Paco stumbled into the silo, Peter saw Marisa outlined in the light, heard her shocked cry.

Blinking, Arastegui lurched past Peter and dropped to the earth beside the nearly naked, unconscious man. Placing his left hand over Ramón's heart, he drew a revolver from his uniform holster and pointed it at Peter.

"Now," he said in a deadly voice, "you will tell me why you have done this thing."

SEVENTEEN

Marisa was staring in horror at the wooden case, at the body of the man beside it. She was wearing khaki shirt and skirt and a blue *boina*, and it came irrelevantly to Peter that she looked more like a Girl Guide than the Royalists' Joan of Arc.

"Tell him," Peter said.

With an effort she drew her gaze from the scene and shrank from him. *"No,"* she said hoarsely. "Oh no!" Unbelievingly. Then she shuddered.

"Talk!" Paco snarled. Then a lean, tall figure came through the doorway, and Peter saw that it was Carbajal.

"Marisa," Peter began, and saw the loathing in her face as she turned to face Podret.

"You lied to me!" she cried. "You said you could help him. You've tried to kill him!"

"Marisa," said Podret. "Listen to me. It is over now, and he is not harmed."

"What did you do to him?"

"We—I continued the therapy that began with building the *isba*. This"—he gestured at the wooden box—"is a *sobatschnik*. We built it together. Your—he has been in them many times before."

"But *why*?" she blurted. "How could you be so cruel?"

Grimacing, Podret glanced nervously at Paco's gun. "We had to re-create an episode in his life," he said simply.

"*Fraud!*" Carbajal rasped suddenly, and moved toward the recorder, but Podret grasped it first. Halting, Carbajal stared furiously at Peter. "Get out!" he screamed. *"Get out!"*

Peter shook his head. He said to Marisa, "He is a Soviet agent. The recorder—" But as he spoke, Carbajal scrambled over to where Ramón Baeza lay, pushed Arastegui aside, and knelt beside the unconscious man.

There was something in his hand, Peter saw; something black and cylindrical that he held against Ramón's bare chest. Lunging past a startled Paco, Peter kicked at Carbajal's wrist and saw a blast of flame shoot outward, heard the deafening report, the smack of a slug on stone. Yelping, Carbajal fell sideways, clutching his wrist, as Peter pivoted and wrenched the revolver from Paco's hand.

He tossed the revolver to Podret, bent over and scooped up the black metal tube. Less than four inches long, it resembled a thick fountain pen, but it was a one-shot Stinger; deadly when fired into a man's spine—or heart.

To Paco he snapped, "Bring Carbajal," and walked toward the doorway.

"But—" Marisa faltered, "I don't *understand.*"

"Then listen to the tape."

Podret said, "Yes, Marisa. When you hear it you will understand—and no one else need know." Placing the recorder on the case, he reset the reels and turned on the switch.

Arastegui was helping Carbajal from the dirt floor. Peter went out to his car, started the engine, and waited while the two men walked slowly toward it, Carbajal moaning in pain.

They took Carbajal to the *bodega* under the main house. He refused to answer Peter's questions until Arastegui threatened to strangle him. Then the Movement's *impulsor* admitted that he had been under Soviet control since 1936 when, seized by the Madrid OGPU, he had begun working for Major Verardini in return for his life. Posing as a member of the Nationalist underground, Carbajal had funneled refugees into Cheka prisons, and since none survived Carbajal was never denounced. The Soviets, he said, forced him to continue working under threat of revealing his Civil War treachery. He did not know if Klaus Ehrlich was Volkov; he knew only that Ehrlich was a ranking officer of the GRU. Beatriz Peralta had been born of Spanish parents in the U.S.S.R.; he did not know her real name; Ehrlich called her Lydia. Sainz had been killed because he knew Rodrigo had an illegitimate half-brother and might have exposed the impersonation.

Carbajal gave Peter a list of nine Soviet illegal and Spanish Communist agents in Spain—together with their locations and signal plans. His code pads and transmitter were concealed in his house behind a panel at the head of his bed. Ehrlich had fled, he said, accompanied by Beatriz; Carbajal denied that he knew how they had left Spain or where they had gone.

The impersonation plan had begun four years before, when

it had become apparent that neither Sainz nor Marisa would countenance Royalist violence against the government. Intimates of the count had been disposed of at calculated intervals lest the Soviet assassination program become suspect—with Professor Sainz the final liquidation target after the pseudo-count was back in Spain. Then, with Ramón a controlled agent, accepted as the returned count, both Carbajal and the Soviets were confident of provoking an uprising. If it succeeded, the Royalist leaders were to be quickly replaced with agents who would convert Spain into a Soviet bastion in Western Europe. If the uprising failed—as was generally assumed—the government could be depended upon to eradicate the Royalists root and branch, removing a persistent source of anti-Soviet hostility. Either outcome offered the Kremlin substantial profit.

"But," said Arastegui as they left the *bodega*, "neither will happen—thanks to you."

Peter looked at his watch. There was no air service from Lérida; he would have to drive to Madrid.

"Keep a watch on Carbajal."

"Of course. But what will we do with him?"

"The Madrid police should be able to think of something. If they can't, the Soviets will." He entered the house, Paco at his heels. In his room he began to pack, Paco watching from the bed, and as he closed his suitcase the Spaniard said, "You are going to Madrid?"

"Yes."

He grimaced. "Will you return?"

Peter glanced through the window at the barrier of green trees, at the fields and sunburned hills beyond. "I don't know," he said slowly. He lifted the suitcase, but Paco took it from him. "Please," the Spaniard said. "For me it is an honor."

Peter smiled. So much in the Spanish character he thought; extravagantly quick to love or hate, so courtly in contrition.

As they went down the stairway Paco said, "What of Ramón Baeza, Pedro?"

"He carries Marisa's blood in his veins. Ramón is the half-brother of her father—her uncle." Pushing open the door, Peter hurried toward the Mercedes. "He deserves your pity—and your care."

"Yes," the colonel said, and when he had placed the suitcase in the rear of the car he pulled off his weapons belt, and took the *boina* from his head. "I think," he said wistfully, "that we have dreamed a dream too long. Like children, perhaps."

Peter said nothing.

"There is the Spain of legend, Pedro; the Spain of yesterday. There is the Spain of today . . . and the Spain of tomorrow." Sadly he gazed at his polished belt, the battle beret in his hands. "I think what we should do today is prepare ourselves for the Spain of tomorrow—the Spain of our children and their children."

"Because," said Peter, "you are a brave and honest man, you will know what to do."

They shook hands then. Arastegui ran one hand through his silvery hair, and blinked as moisture welled in his eyes. Peter put the car in gear and steered around the house.

Looking back, he saw a plume of dust in the distance where Marisa would be driving back to the house. With Ramón, he thought, Sol Podret, and—the precious tape recorder. Turning back, he steered for the main road, reached it, accelerated the Mercedes, and held the speedometer needle steadily at 80 as the road to Lérida unwound.

It was early evening when he reached the outskirts of Madrid, dusk when he turned onto Maldonado. There were no roadblocks shutting off the street, no lantern-strung barriers. And from where he parked the car he could see no traces of the trenches the police had filled.

He went to the door and rang the bell, and as he waited he sensed that he had done all this before: the door would open on Estanislao and he would enter and walk back to a room where Beatriz and Ehrlich waited with expressions on their faces he would remember the rest of his life.

The street was quiet. No cars passed, and the only sound was the rumble of distant traffic, the evensong of birds.

No one answered the bell.

He rang again, then tried the door, and saw it open inward.

The corridor was as he remembered it—dark and musty, with the scent of old decay. In the dimness he found the stairs and mounted them, going from one room to another until he reached one with an oak double door. Turning the brass handle, he pulled it open, and it moved as silently as a wraith of smoke. Inside, the room was nearly dark, the shutters closed, the heavy draperies drawn.

He walked toward the rumpled bed and halted. A pillow angled upward, and as he stared he saw the twisted outlines of a body from which a slip had been torn.

She lay there waxlike in her nakedness, and when he touched her wrist it was cold. The hairs behind his neck lifted as he pushed away the pillow and saw her cyanosed, contorted face. The eyes were bloodshot where capillaries had broken in her final agony. He closed them gently and smoothed her features with his hand.

She had fought well against the smothering pillow, for

there was bloodstained tissue under her clawing nails. The lighter flame burned low, and he glimpsed a sheet of paper placed between her loins.

Turning on the bed lamp, he held the paper so that he could read the coarse Cyrillic writing, and as he read he translated:

Lydia Mirovna
A Soviet Citizen
Who would have betrayed the Socialist
Fatherland

Below it, the single letter *V*.

Her epitaph, he thought broodingly, composed by her executioner. Closing his eyes, he shook himself, drew in a deep breath, and let the paper flutter to the bed.

As he tapped the paneled wall he tried not to look at the body of the woman he had known as Beatriz Peralta, but he could not help glimpsing it. The shrunken breasts and twisted limbs formed an obscene caricature of the *Maja Desnuda*; no roseate warmth and invitation; a stark and waxen horror.

His knuckles rapped, and the sound of hollow depth reverberated. Stepping back, he examined the panel, knowing that there would be concealed access, and knowing also that he had no time to spend in search.

A poker from the fireplace splintered the wood: he pried enough from the cache so that he could take out a small pad of onionskin covered by cheap reddish paper. Then he felt for the transmitter and drew out a metal box no larger than a margarine container.

Holding it in his hand for a moment, he gazed at it and the code pad and thought that these were the prizes of a covert operation, the final goals of efforts in which a thousand men would join before the end was achieved. A penny's worth of paper, he mused, and a quarter's worth of metal—nothing more.

Pocketing them, he turned toward the bed with its alabaster burden, and thought that if what he had found was the prize, what lay before him was the price. Beatriz and Don Eduardo, José Perdomo, Estanislao, and Pablo. Even Carbajal.

All the factors of the equation had been false; only the solution was correct.

He turned off the lamp to shroud the girl in darkness, closed the room of death, and went out to the street and his car.

Without looking back.

That night from his apartment he transmitted a long Priority to Headquarters, and his orders came early in the morning.

Sol returned at noon, dusty and disheveled. Handing over the tape of their psychodrama to Peter, he said, "Going somewhere? Bags packed, I see. Curtains drawn."

"Nonstop to New York." Peter mixed a short Canadian Club and drank it bottoms-up.

"Well, well," Podret murmured. "What does that mean?"

"Whatever you want it to."

"I see. We hadn't thought you'd be leaving quite so soon."

"We?"

"Marisa and your humble servant—but principally Marisa. She wants to see you, Peter. You might assume that."

"There isn't time," he said. "They're waiting for me at New York Airport. NSA's alerted to process the code pad." Grimacing, he pulled out his pipe, thrust it back in his pocket, and poured a finger of whiskey. "What are you going to do?"

"I'm going back to the *finca*."

Peter set down his glass. "Then you can explain things to Marisa."

"What things? I'm going back to take care of Ramón another week or so. He knows who he is now. Most of the rest I blotted out. I'll stay with him and guard against relapse."

"Does she know who I am—my work?"

"She's an intelligent woman, Peter. She hasn't actually spoken the magic initials, but she's come to realize that hardly anything happens spontaneously—that what you and I were able to accomplish requires organization and extraordinary resources."

"That makes it easier."

"Not on her."

"In time it will. Her life is here, Sol: Madrid and Catalonia—"

"And you're the Seraph—the Man from Everywhere." Sol's tongue made a sucking noise against his teeth. "Peter, take a later plane. I can have her here in—"

But Peter shook his head. "It's a frayed old scene, Sol: the customary table in their usual café—the discreet and understanding waiter who brings their favorite wine. They toast, he kisses her hand and trudges off while she watches through tear-filled eyes. . . ."

Podret shook his head. "It doesn't have to play that way."

"For now it does."

"Then I hope you remember her—and miss her."
"I will," he said, shook his friend's hand, and carried his bags down to the street.

EIGHTEEN

From his poolside chair Peter gazed out over Zihuatanejo Bay with the beach and the opalescent Pacific beyond. Southeast, toward Acapulco, the hook of Petatlán thrust into the ocean, a sheltering mole for small sailing and fishing boats. Hull down on the glistening horizon, a Panama-bound tramp smudged the pale blue sky with its smoke.

There were palms behind him, and a *primavera* tree from whose branches, slothlike, hung the pet coati of his hostess, shaded from the morning sun.

She lay in the emerald pool, drifting in a white float chair, plastic cups across her eyelids, the rest of her brown body nearly naked to the sun. The drink tray at her hand held the dregs of a tequila Bloody Mary.

Peter's fork speared another slice of iced papaya plucked that morning from a hillside tree, and as he sipped *café con leche* he watched Patty wriggle from her float and disappear under the surface of the pool.

Idly his gaze followed her, a caramel-colored water sprite darting over the tinted tiles. When she surfaced she splashed and streaked his colored glasses. How different her vibrant, electric body, he thought, from the pallid, waxen corpse he had left in the house on Maldonado Street.

"A peso for your thoughts," she teased, wrinkling her gamin nose.

"They're worth less than a centavo." Pushing his plate aside, he went to the edge of the pool.

He had left Madrid a week before, and three days at Langley had wrapped up his Spanish saga. Carbajal's transmitter proved to be a recent model and of considerable interest to the people who handled—and intercepted—agent radio traffic. The code pad was current and NSA looked forward to decoding a good many GRU-agent messages before the system changed.

As for Ehrlich, MI-6 reported the illegal arrival and arrest in Gibraltar of a man whose West German passport identified him as Klaus Ehrlich. The prisoner declined to explain his presence in Gibraltar until threatened with deportation to Bonn, after which he placed a call to the Soviet embassy in London. The embassy thereupon demanded that the Foreign Office grant diplomatic immunity to Colonel Sergei N. Volkov, whose fraudulent documentation the embassy did not bother to explain. The Foreign Office rejected the embassy demand but ordered the release of Volkov in the custody of the Soviet consul in Gibraltar, after which he was seen no more.

Mild treatment for a terrorist and murderer, Peter had reflected, and less inconvenience to Volkov than an underdone three-minute egg. For the Spets Byuro, the failure of Volkov's mission could be taken in stride. Including Lydia Mirovna and Carbajal, their eventual loss would be eleven *agenturniy rabotniki,* probably no more than a fraction of their clandestine assets in Spain, and there would be others pipelined to take their places.

So it goes on, Peter thought; the endless wash of espionage, like the ebb and flow of a secret, subterranean sea.

"I'm so glad you came, Peter," Patty murmured, and sloshed water over his hands. "Was Madrid a disappointment?"

"Why?"

"Oh, you seem so preoccupied, detached. And every day you're restless until Juanito brings your Spanish paper." She looked up at him and her eyes were serious. "Unfinished business? Something left behind?"

"In a way," he admitted. He slipped into the pool and swam with her until the white-coated houseboy came out to the pool with an airmail copy of *ABC*.

Leaving the pool, Peter sat in the shade and scanned the pages for provincial news. But what he was looking for was on the front page, with photographs and a boldface headline: THE COUNT OF PRADOS RENOUNCES HIS CLAIMS TO THE THRONE, then the lead: ROYALIST MOVEMENT DISBANDS.

He read the text quickly. A review of Royalist partisans by the Conde de Prados had culminated in an address in which the count renounced all pretensions to the throne of his ancestors, declared the Royalist Movement dissolved, and urged his followers to work within the traditional institutions of Spain.

His statement had come as a shock to the Royalists, many of whom began to shout angrily at the count. Order, however, was maintained by Coronel Francisco Arastegui, after which the women were addressed by the young *condesa*.

Photographs showed her standing on an open platform erected before a round stone building that Peter recognized as the silo. She wore no Royalist beret, only the simple khaki shirt and blouse in which he had last seen her. Her hair flowed loosely over her shoulders, and he thought that it must have been a trick of the lighting, for he had never seen her look so young. So beautiful.

Or so desirable.

For a time he sat there, gazing unseeingly at the paper before him, his thoughts half a world away. He saw her in mourning, in her cocktail dress, her white ruffled blouse; he remembered the appeal of her sweet smile. He felt her hand on his, the slaking touch of her lips, and wondered whether he would ever feel their softness again.

Then Patty's voice broke into his thoughts, and he rose, stepped into leather sandals, and walked beside her down to the golden sand.

Part V

While his horse grazed the grassy hillside, the man from Vorkuta lay back and felt the sun-soaked earth warm his body.

It was a peaceful place, he thought, a place of contentment; with the azure sky above and below the soil of Catalonia where peasants tended their watered fields. The good land freed them from the serfdom he had fought against so long ago, and as he watched men working with their wives and children, he sorrowed for others he had left behind—prisoners of the endless, blinding prostor; *wretched slaves in* siblags *and frozen forests.*

His horse moved forward, reins trailing in the grass, and a frightened partridge whirred wildly from its nest, up and away, gliding on outspread wings to some hidden sanctuary farther down the hill.

Where he had come from there had been no birds, no broods of partridge in the rich spring grass; no songs at evening or at dawn. He had come from a place where the air itself was death to a place where the sun shone, the land gave birth, and seasons changed slowly. And here he had found a name, a family, and a home, and had learned the truth that compassion was humanity and humanity was life itself.

Beyond the hill sheep moved, and the chime of their soft bells was soothing to his ears. Droning bees hovered above a clump of yellow wild flowers, and he thought of sweet honey in the wintertime, of milk and cheese and the good things of the earth.

In the months and years ahead there was much he could do: help men and women work their fields, foal mares and calve the cows, and build what was needed with his axe and mallet and saw.

It would be a good life, he told himself, a useful life, and there was satisfaction in work done of one's own free will.

His horse lifted her head and nickered, and he saw below another horse with rider, a slim straight girl whose flat Andalusian hat bounced behind her shoulders. Marisa, he thought, whose blood I share, and then he faced south toward Borjas, where the grave of his mother lay.

He remembered her from his childhood, saw clearly her dark and gentle face, felt the comforting strength of her arms, and knew that he would stay here in the land of her people for the remainder of his life.

Tears welled in his eyes and spilled down his rough cheeks as he rose to his knees, bowed his head, and in humble gratitude began to pray.